THE CUBAN MILE

THE CUBAN MILE

BY

ALEJANDRO HERNÁNDEZ DÍAZ

TRANSLATED FROM THE SPANISH BY
DICK CLUSTER

Latin American Literary Review Press
Series: Discoveries
1998

The Latin American Literary Review Press publishes Latin American creative writing under the series title Discoveries, and critical works under the series title Explorations.

Library of Congress Cataloging-in-Publication Data

Hernández Díaz, Alejandro, 1970-
    [Milla. English]
    The Cuban mile / by Alejandro Hernández Díaz ; translated from the Spanish by Dick Cluster.
             p.   cm. -- (Series Discoveries)
        ISBN 0-935480-94-3
        I. Cluster, Dick, 1947- . II. Title. III. Series: Discoveries.
PQ7390.H396M5513   1998
863--dc21
                                    98-5433
                                       CIP

The paper used in this publication meets the minimum requirements of the American National Standard for Permanence of Paper for Printed Library Materials Z39.48-1984.∞

Latin American Literary Review Press
121 Edgewood Avenue
Pittsburgh, PA 15218

Translator's Note

Cuban writer and critic Leonardo Padura once told me that he had read somewhere how North Americans tend to see Cuba with one eye only—usually, one of condemnation, and occasionally, one of worship. I am happy to bring Alejandro Hernández Díaz's novel to an English readership in the U.S. in part because I think it will provide those readers with a more binocular vision of Cuba. In addition, readers in the U.S. and Canada rarely have the opportunity to read publications written by and for Cubans living on the island. My hope is that this work, originally written and published in Havana, will begin to fill that immense gap.

I have footnoted culturally specific references in the text that may not be clear to those unfamiliar with Cuban culture. In only a few cases have I inserted information directly into the text to avoid a burdensome number of footnotes. Otherwise, I have tried to render the narrator's voice (showy at times to native Cubans and foreigners alike) as faithfully as possible.

Many people have assisted me in creating this translation. It has benefitted from the careful scrutiny of Fabiola Carratalá throughout, and from explanations of particular mysteries by Tony González and Justo Vasco. Salim Handatjaia brought me and Alejandro Hernández together. My Cuban friends, students and teachers who assisted me in understanding their country are too many to name, but they know who they are. Reyes Coll-Tellechea has been an inimitable guide to my continuing study of the Spanish language and its literature.

FIRST DAY
7:19 P.M.

Swathed in his camouflage outfit, facing me with feet planted and hands on hips, the Commodore reminds me of the old movie about the Colossus of Rhodes that I liked so much in elementary school. That ashen stone idol and bearer of the fire of the gods who succumbed to their power incarnate in a tidal wave, and so lost the homage of centuries to come. I picture this replica, with his Greek athlete's body, collapsing at a single stroke into jagged pieces to be swallowed up by the sea. Defeated just like his predecessor by the elements' rage. He doesn't know how ridiculous he looks struggling to keep his balance astride a little boat full of knapsacks, offering me such a poetic image with the sun setting at his back— worthy of the best animators in Japan. His face smiles as if it were announcing "At last," because with the disappearance of the final gray outlines of the coast begins our adventure—a term he does not like. Now he lowers himself to his post in the stern, intent on thinking hard, reflecting on his life lived thus far, to arrive at the present moment with the slogan "Born Again!" An excellent way to relieve us of any past guilt and reassure us that everything will be better from here on out. God, I can't deny it, this is impressive. I've got goose pimples. Hundreds of trumpets ought be sounding somewhere above to do justice to the pompous air of this ceremony. At least, I can imagine them. They echo in my brain, making me believe my future is a yellow brick road strewn with laurel leaves. The truth is, though, that I lack this marvelous ability to rev myself up in anticipation of hallelujahs. When I think of the future, my stomach fails me and I get this goddamn diarrhea that wipes out any desire to build castles in the air. That's why I don't pay any attention to palm readers who pretend to tell your fortune through a formulaic recitation of possibilities that seem to be copied from cookbook recipes. I've accepted my life—and I'm only twenty-one—without any great to-do. According to the Commodore this makes me an apathetic type, but that's not true. It's just that I can't start rambling on about my fabulous future to come when right now, on an insignificant day in July, it's almost dark and I'm surrounded by water on all sides.

MILE 5

This Commodore business, I just say it to bother him. His name is Angel, and the nickname is because he knows so much about the sea. His pals in the navy gave it to him when he was a sergeant, second class, and spent his nights at the breakwaters of the coast imagining galleons and sailing ships. Physically, he's a typical sailor of the tropics: swarthy, formidably muscular, his hair bleached by the sun. He loves porno films full of lesbians and the macho pronouncements of Vargas Vila.[1] He dances a magnificent *casino*, listens to the Pasteles Verdes,[2] and his motto is "Within the same hands that I lift you to heaven, I have the strength to plunge you back into the muck." Nonetheless, behind all this big-balls exterior he clothes himself in, he's not a bad guy. It's just too bad he's my sister's sex symbol, because having such a macho-man as a kind of brother-in-law isn't exactly something to be thankful for. His most positive trait is his passion. Of the four character types outlined by Pavlov, he enjoys the well-balanced "strong, full-blooded" one, much desired by ninety-nine percent of my friends. This allows him to get excited, to be moved, without onerous aftereffects. A luxury, a true luxury in a world where good and evil are off partying, and sentimentalism is a cliched image of a hero and heroine kissing to the song from *Casablanca*.

Since we first met, we've confronted a very obvious incompatibility. It's all very well to share a game of dominoes on a Saturday afternoon, or watch a Chinese movie like *New Adventures of the Ninja*, but it's another thing entirely to spend three months laughing at

[1] José María Vargas Vila: a prolific, early-twentieth-century Colombian poet and novelist, known in Cuba for his misogynist verses.
[2] Pasteles Verdes: a Venezuelan rock group.

the same Alvarez Guedes[3] cassette, protesting between chuckles and tears that the guy is fantastic, he really is. My sister deserves something better. She's got smarts and a body both, and to spare. I'd bet anything the Commodore only satisfies her libidinal needs. Sailors have a reputation for embedding pearls in their pricks to drive women crazy, or if it's not that, they must feed them some of those potions praised at length by dirty old men in dry dock cultivating their last confessions. Plenty of women are satisfied with this. I'm not saying my sister is one of them, it's just that she needs someone outside the academic formalities that surround her at the university. The more I look at him, the more convinced I am of their differences. Right now he's stretched out in the stern like a hog.

By now he must be bored with trying to come up with ideas, and he's dreaming of the oceans of neon signs along the streets of Miami. Smile, smile you bastard and enjoy the mediocre ideal of sipping Coke and Bacardi while you sit at a bar in Little Havana trading lies with Sylvester Stallone. Yes my man, you'll tell him, they can criticize you all they want. But I say, there's no better teacher than a good kick in the ass.

---

[3] Alvarez Guedes: a Cuban-American comedian who imitates Cuban mannerisms and speech.

MILE 7

It's getting dark. For the first time, I can see night fall in a setting that's nearly absolute—the broad ocean dyed gray by the sky, and then finally dyed black. Since I was kid I've heard the saying, "The sea is the reflection of the sky; cloudy sky, cloudy sea." So I would look in vain for the white areas where the nimbuses might rest. It was as if there were no room for white. Blue and green, yes, the flag-bearers of some remote origin replete with contrasts, and black, of course, being the maximum inspirer of fear. And I can feel that now, because the falling darkness carries with it this first fear that begins with a queasiness in the stomach or an erection down below. My heart jumps at the slightest sound, giving rise to a certain sensation of helplessness. Welcome to the fear. When was the last time you felt this excitement? It reminds me of that children's game where you walk along the top of a wall imagining different but equally terrible deaths waiting on each side. There was a brief moment, just before you fell, when it didn't matter one iota that the whole thing was an act, and right then I'd be overcome by a true panic, a split second of horror that was exactly what I was after every time. What I'm starting to experience now is the stretching-out of that instant, a prolongation which I'll have to feed with my worst expectations, because here there are no second tries, and a fall—well, a fall or no fall will be a question of luck.

My first day at sea. The first day of being nobody. It seems to me that I can't really count myself as someone as long as I remain outside of the usual circles that dictate custom. I prefer the title of hybrid—and in fact that's what I am—while crossing this watery limbo which may, perhaps, teach me not to criticize the civilized land-dwelling ones too much, in spite of all the spite they may deserve. And this is an example of the things that don't bother the Commodore. "To be or not to be," that's not his question. Who knows, maybe this is another reason women use to justify succumbing to his charms. I'm even a little jealous of this characteristic myself.

MILE 8

It's understandable that I can't fall asleep
till late at night. A long parade of thoughts marches
through my gray matter, forbidding any pause for relax-
ation, despite twenty-some tired hours now. There are
the echoes of the "See you soon" which wasn't spoken,
the "Take care of yourself," the "See you over there."
There's the smell of the leaves in my house in Vedado
on those early Sunday mornings when the neighbors
played the latest Jerry Rivera record to accompany the
weekly house cleaning, and the old ladies across the street
complained about the bread, because every day the bakers were stealing more and more, and my father invited
me to read the center spread of *Rebel Youth* so I could
learn how Napoleon Bonaparte's last doctor came to
Cuba to die. All this was yesterday. Yesterday stayed
behind, on the other side, together with twenty years of
Sundays. Not even a farewell, no, it's much worse this
way. Maybe it saves them grief, but at the price of having to review my past with the melodrama of a soap opera. I'm gripped by terrible nostalgia and I cry for the
leaves, the neighbors, the old women and the bakers,
and even for Napoleon, who died attended by the doctor
my father told me about.

To distract myself from this premature
melancholy, I invite the Commodore to play cards under
a flashlight. We play poker, the pastime of Western tough
guys and Chicago gangsters. North America loves a full
house with aces as much it loves flags on the Fourth of
July. All my life that's what I've seen on my television
screen, which also convinced me that what reigned over
there was the chaos of YES-YOU-CAN (the mischie-
vous character who turned a city upside-down in that

cartoon *Made in the CCCP*) while Cuba was personified by his opposite character, NO-YOU-CAN'T, with that annoyed expression, always relying on good sense, on proletarian logic, lining the nation up to move toward a tedious, well-balanced future without either Superman or Pepsi-Cola. And so—these Marxists are really not so practical—the North became entwined with my fantasies of the Magi, the Three Kings who would bestow on me the wonders of that country of chaos, of the all-possible with its magazines full of Mickey Mouse. That was my childhood trench in the class struggle...At the end of the last hand I ask my valiant captain how far he thinks we've gone. He moves his head as if he isn't sure, but he declares, "Far. By now, we've gone far."

SECOND DAY
9:20 A.M.

MILE 13

As I get my shipwrecked self up on this beautiful morning, I am surprised by an impressive expanse of Gulf which has left its innocent colors behind. I'm not sure that's the best word to describe the sobriety of the sea. What I mean is, we're done with the cute tropical blue of the beaches and the Caribbean green of a painter's wash. Now there's a bottomless color, a blue-gray-violet which covers the far-off seafloor of strange aquarium fish, of who knows how many ships and skeletons clothed in coral, diamonds, precious stones and silenced guns. They say there's also a telephone cable down there which used to connect the island with the continent. For all I know, I'm sailing right over the site where Camilo's[4] crashed airplane lies. Who knows, it all belongs to this Gulf which is as docile at it is damned; today it shows you one of its secrets, tomorrow you be-

[4] Camilo Cienfuegos: a leading rebel officer along with Fidel Castro and Che Guevara, and then commander of the army; he died in an airplane crash in October 1959.

come another one of its trophies on the wall. But the difference is not only in the color; the current's force is more evident, and the waves—with good weather still— rock us back and forth and splash us with salt. It wouldn't be hard for me to turn around, it's an alternative there for the taking, but I'd hate to have to handle the argument with my conscience which, once rescued, wouldn't pardon me. Yes, because the burden of shame isn't a revolutionary lie to get people to endure another three months on the barricades and chant "They shall not cross" or "Fatherland or death, victory is ours." This burden lies with the idiot who got four stab wounds for refusing to give up his watch, with the husband who never hurt a fly, but one day chopped up his wife with a machete for cheating on him, or the man who went off sailing, tasting one fear after another, one after another, until finally he couldn't turn back. I once met a general who said that bravery was just the rare circumstance in which fear caused you to run forward. So, a hero is a coward blessed by the occasion, while the rest are consistently chicken.

The Commodore is up, more talkative than usual. First he's advising me to keep on the straw hat that he traded a pair of glasses for in Quivicán.[5] Also, I should treat my skin three times a day with an anti-dehydration sunscreen. Next he'll start a conversation/ monologue about the Gulf Stream, detailing all the information and approximations needed to embark on a one hundred and fifty kilometer trip, and how the slightest oversight can lead to us being carried to doubtful places where we'd be harder to find than a flea in an Olympic swimming pool. According to studies done at the University of Florida, the chances of rescue during the first six days are fifty percent. After that they drop by five percent a day, from which I can deduce that after two weeks at sea the only solution is to go on floating

---

[5] Quivicán: a town in the rural province of Havana.

longer and longer and longer. Showing off my much-criticized imperturbability, I ask the Colossus for his sea-dog's opinion, because I want to hear, again, his self-assured words marked with the pride of those who live convinced that this—crossing the seas—is what they know best. He'll say, "It's going great." And that way I'll feel a little happier. Without a doubt he's the one who knows this business, and I'll hurry to put on my blessed hat, spray my arms and neck with the protectant, squeeze my body into the bow, and stay out of his way.

       These Air Force rafts are a marvel; the air is compartmentalized in five separate chambers and the raft comes supplied with a manual air pump, emergency patches, and collapsible aluminum oars. The Commodore checks our heading every half-hour with a compass. First, he carefully observes the needle, then the sky, and then the sea. My duty is to scan the horizon for whatever might be there. The screaming red color of the raft makes it stand out at a distance, which can be either good or bad, depending on who finds us. I make myself comfortable among the knapsacks that contain—separately—the water, the food, and my favorite books. I had to sweat bricks to get the Commodore to take on those sixteen volumes. He said they were useless weight and even promised to get me other and better ones when he collected his first American paycheck. It would have done the trick if I had explained that just three or four of them would cost a week's worth of food, but instead I told him they were important to have on board because they were my good-luck charms, as well as a useful way to avoid the debilitating stress that silence can bring.

MILE 14

Our raft has been christened. The day before we left, I asked "my captain" whether it wouldn't be a good omen to give the boat a name. He was happy to say yes, and right away began to think of the names best-loved by fishermen: Lucky, the Islet, Virgin Mary, Siren II. He even thought of my sister's name: Cynthia. Which doesn't sound bad, but frighteningly kitsch. I wanted something more creative, more classical, so I decided to christen her *The Social Contract*. To the Commodore's disconsolate face, I explained that I'd once heard a certain Cuban writer speak of a sailing ship which, during the time of the French Revolution, had travelled the world with this title carved into its prow in order to spread the ideas of Jean Jacques Rousseau to every port.

"And what the fuck am I supposed to care about this Roso?" he duly blurted out.

"To me it sounds pretty," I said. "It sounds liberating, and at least it would be an allegory of good luck."

He tried to argue some half-baked points: It sounded like something fashionable among artists and gays, or a humorless intellectual joke that had nothing to do with us. When you looked at it closely didn't this old ship's name bear some resemblance to communist slogans? Finally, though, he had to accept my proposal because he hadn't come up with anything better, and I refused to sail in any craft with a kitschy name. It was enough having lived my twenty years in a country where all the stores are called "Friendship" and everybody wears the same shoes. Even though he couldn't understand this, I don't think my companion is so dumb. His problem doesn't stem from how little he knows, but from the shitload of things he's not interested in. For him, happiness is a pretty girl—and my sister is that—and living close to the sea with a television set to entertain him twice a week with movies full of shoot-outs and karate kicks. He's heading for Florida idealizing Anglo-Saxon asses and free sex like on American Ecstasy, the porn channel. So, Rousseau doesn't count for much. He's a sad case. It's enough to see him seated in the bow searching for north on the compass. I'll never forget the night we met. After the "how-are-you's" and "pleased-to-meet-you's," we got together over some cane liquor to chat about love in times of siege, and upon hearing me confess my devotion to painting, he assured me smugly that painting was a job for bisexuals. That was the only thing that could explain the artist's indifference to the tantalizing nudity of his models—as if I occupied myself painting nothing but busty virgins here in the last days of a millennium satiated with mail-order orgasms, AIDS, and virtual reality. I laughed for quite a while and then showed him some of my canvasses, which he'll never understand, while what I didn't know was that I was in the presence of the one chosen to take me to the land of wonders, where the elite are accustomed to celebrating success in spacious galleries over sliced turkey and caviar. The artist will visit those precincts that stole from Paris the sovereignty of the art world and shifted it to the city of skyscrapers. Ode to the flags of Jasper Johns and the ambiguities of Rauschenberg. I'm going to announce myself with a style that has escaped the West for thirty years, all the while having warded off the blows of its state sponsors as well. The priceless merit of the bohemians of San Alejandro.[6] Navigating among the idols of American postmodernism, the sacred cows of the Metropolitan Museum, I'll be the new patriarch of the set-

---

[6] San Alejandro: a prestigious public high school in Havana dedicated to the visual arts.

tees and the appreciative smile, with a saucer full of olives in my right hand and a glass of Chivas Regal at my lips to soak my pompous speech of opposition to Socialist Realism in the flavor of barrel-aged scotch whiskey. What total bullshit! No, I don't make such ridiculous plans, which only land you at the age of forty spouting decadent monologues in your favorite bar blaming a state of exile that never asked you to come to it, or transforming into the conservative who delivers passionate dissertations about the sanctity of the family and the morality of Socrates. My captain, in the end, wasn't even interested in asking who Jean Jacques Rousseau was. I would have told him, really I would have, that Rousseau isn't any big deal.

MILE 17

The morning has passed quickly. There's a splendid sun which reddens my skin, eluding the chemical snares so praised by the Commodore. This damn rocking continues, up and down like on a merry-go-round...If we had brought a sail we'd be making better time...If the raft had wings, it could fly. Better not dwell on *if*s...Beautiful day, barely a couple of clouds. I think I could get used to the Gulf. I'm less afraid than yesterday, this is what I call "getting warmed up." Tomorrow I'll be an expert, capable of distinguishing the shape of a school of sardines from one of tuna, except first they have to show up, because so far I haven't seen a single flash of fish scales in this fucking Caribbean Sea.

MILE 18

I'm reading. First I tried to lose myself in Conan Doyle's world with *The Hound of the Baskervilles*, but thrillers don't work in a state of forced uncertainty; instead of providing you with an escape they only expedite your despair. On the other hand, with historical works the epic spirit of past actions soaks into your pores and stimulates sacrifice—not just five days under a frightful sun, but a whole month, searing yourself for the greater glory of humanity like a hermit in love with self-flagellation...No joking, I think that living through an experience like this is a privilege, it lets me rub shoulders with death. I see death in the movement of the water. I feel its touch in the luminous glow that's cooking my flesh. It's a warm death, a reflection born out of the great blue...In the twelfth canto of *The Odyssey*, the Sun says, "I will sink to the abode of Hades, and light up the dead." That's the right kind of book for the voyage. It propels me, firing up my consciousness with a battle cry: "Onward, argonaut. Thy fleece awaits!"

MILE 19

At last, lunch on the high seas: rolls with canned ham and chocolate bars. The Commodore says this is the combat diet of pilots. He spent more than two months investigating the quantity of calories needed in emergency situations, and he's satisfied that he's assembled the right nutrients for us. Chocolate, for example, is a first-class energizer. He tells me that fruits fight off toxins and help establish vitamin equilibrium. Maybe he's just saying this to justify the ten dollars he spent on cans of apples, pears, and peaches, as if our domestic fruits were accomplices in Marxism and would poison those who had abandoned their fields...With respect to water, we have to consume one and a half cups at each meal, and another one in between. The Commodore—obviously—can bear this regimen more easily than I can. In the army he got used to drinking the minimum, and it wouldn't surprise me if he spent his last days in Cuba practicing stoicism on the beaches of Marianao. In my case, the sun bakes my blood; right away I've got a dry mouth, my skin is irritated, and my head throbs painfully. I could drink two liters a day. The Moroccan soldiers who guard King Hassan's Saharan walls are supplied with only three liters a week. And that's really worse, because desert thirst plus war makes for total martyrdom. So I'm making an effort—so far it's not too hard—to withdraw into the soliloquy of my books and leave behind my accumulated appetites. The Colossus thinks there must be something strange behind my ability to concentrate on reading without the motion of the waves making me nauseous. Really, I got used to it long ago, thanks to the impossible fortnightly trips with my father to visit relatives in Batabanó. Whether by milk train or by car, I immersed myself in the adventure books of Salgari, the crossword puzzles in *Bohemia*, or an old comic about The Thing rescuing Chinamen from the empire of Mao. I never felt much nausea, except when it came disguised in vapors of ethanol. So I feel sorry for my sister's boyfriend, unaware of the pleasure of avoiding boredom, seeing the same thing over and over again. Flying fish are the only fauna showing themselves out here. They appear and vanish by the dozens, thrown forward meter after meter by some strange propulsive mechanism, little missiles guided along the surface of the sea. I ask the Commodore how they taste, and he answers that he's never tried one, but that they're probably nothing to rave about, you probably end up choking on those spiny bones. I also see gulls, arrogant and solitary, showing off in a realm that no one disputes. I can't understand how they are able to orient themselves in this featureless space. To explain marvels of instinct, we always speak of some handy sixth sense. Women turn to it to find out about the infidelities of their men, as does the mother who dreams of the suffering of her prodigal son...and the sea gulls lost in the tricky sea of sardines. The worst is, if one of those sea gulls were to rise a thousand feet over my head, the panorama wouldn't change; it could multiply my limited field of vision by ten and everything would still look the same. It's a terribly irrevocable vision. Too bad I'm not Columbus to deceive myself with a tale of land nearby. The birds saved him, because the hard cases manning his caravels wouldn't have put up with continuing to sail who-knew-where. Five hundred years later the gulls are still in sight, though there are no more mixed-up mariners, so I tell them, "Fly, guys, fly."

MILE 20

What a tedious calm. I propose another hand of poker to the Commodore, but he doesn't seem enthusiastic. "That's a game for assholes," he says, defending dominoes, his beloved pastime, for a thousand afternoons of retirement. My body is burning. I treat my vulnerable parts once more, and change my clothes. In place of the sleeveless t-shirt I donned for the launch, I put on a camouflage shirt that covers my arms—borrowed from my companion on the raft. Up above, the king star reigns, the handsome Phoebus, in the worst hours of the day. It's the afternoon heat, a humid and vicious sea heat, that converts you to an idolatrous worshipper of shade. Salty sweat soaks the skin in droplets which evaporate, leaving behind swellings on a scorched hide. When I close my eyes, my pupils sting. The straw hat is no solution because it heats my brain to ninety degrees Celsius. There is no solution, the best thing is not to obsess, not to watch the splendid sun that takes bites out of me as it pleases, at the hour when my mother always prefers to nap. So I lie down at my post, trying to let my ears be entertained by the delicious and regular tempo of the waves. I know it's something I'm inventing for myself. If you work at it, you can find musicality in anything. There's a heavy metal guitarist who made himself a millionaire with songs inspired by motorcycle noise. A spectrum of melodies is hidden in the apparently boring din, waiting for our auditory patience to create its anthem. And anthem can mean opera, rock, ballad, and even a symphony with *scherzo*, *presto*, and *allegretto*. A symphony born of the vicissitudes of a Cuban emigrant is a great theme for posterity. The essence of revolution has never endured through the ages in a form more moving than that of art. Above the dusty rifles in the display case and the medals of the chief, rises the verdict of the artist. The France that beheaded the Bourbons was universalized by the strains of *La Marseillaise* and the canvas depicting the assassinated Marat. Goya was the Third of May; Emiliano Zapata, a Diego Rivero mural; the Russian October ended up as a mausoleum that hides its mummified leader, while his last followers kneel before the tumbled statues that so poorly eternalized his myth. Cuba is Silvio Rodríguez's *Nueva Trova,*[7] a poem to Camilo Cienfuegos, the famous photo of Che. If I can create my own symphony, I'll be very close to immortality with the thrust of the Revolution backing me up. Anything well made by a Cuban today is a good bet to be imperishable. We're special—the lost tribe of existing socialism, an extinct race.

---

[7] *Nueva Trova*: translated as "New Song," a movement founded by Cuban singer-songwriters Silvio Rodriguez, Pablo Milanés, and others that spread through Latin American in the 1970s.

MILE 22

If only they knew where I was. I didn't keep quiet about it to be discreet, but to surprise them. When you've got a reputation as a man of few words, so common among painters, they tend to underestimate the boldness of your spirit. You're the impossible one, shut up in a room where you imitate the Mona Lisa, smudged all over with acrylics and convinced that this microcosm beats any experience outside. And people pity you because they know it isn't true. It's better to appear crazy. The fundamental difference between the madman and the adventurer is that we pardon the crazy one for his stupidity on account of the sickness of his mind, while the levelheaded adventurer runs the risk of looking like an idiot if his actions fail. In today's world, the madman is admired and the adventurer is scorned. Mel Gibson is the supreme exponent of this—or he was. Millions of women love the neurasthenic policeman who throws himself off roofs, blows buildings to smithereens, and loves dogs and upstanding black men. Whereas the sane hero is a cliche that only works in soap operas.

And in the case of us artists, the public expects lightweight eccentric oddities that uphold the Mel Gibson model so they can say to themselves in the galleries, "He's nothing to write home about, but at least he makes crazy things." Under this aegis, they can justify your who-gives-a-shit behavior, which can be attractive and even explain the extenuating circumstances of your frustration—taking for granted that frustration is what you are suffering from. In fact, you've never worked with this century's aesthetes in mind. You'll start collecting praise within three generations, and fortunately no acquaintance will survive to witness the triumph.

33

Today's madman is tomorrow's genius. When they find out that I'm mixed up in this adventure of exile and navigation, those who don't know me well will say I'm a lunatic bored with dreams of posthumous beatitudes inspired by Van Gogh and Joan of Arc, that I'm an anti-Stendhalist desperate to enjoy the pleasures of the human condition. But my real friends will content themselves with knowing that I'm just one more who left, a number for tomorrow's statistics, that's all.

MILE 24

Night again. Relief. A little while ago we finished eating the same thing we had for lunch: a sandwich with chocolate. I drank two cups of water because of what I'd declined in the afternoon. Now I'm conversing with the Commodore. Really, I'm barely listening, maybe two or three phrases of what he says. I see him in the somber moonlight, shining like a ghost or a maritime satyr who has sprung from the depths of the Gulf in the hopes of chatting with another navigator—myself— so that the insane realism of sky-sea won't give him nightmares. He talks and talks, and to annoy him I don't pay attention. I prefer to look at the gray surroundings and go on enjoying the sound of the sea. The force of the waves has diminished a lot since this morning. There's still some motion, but given the fragility of *The Social Contract*, it's hard to expect less rocking than this. The wind hasn't changed. Well, I don't know anything about it, but I have the impression that it keeps blowing toward the Northeast. How far are we from Key West? If I knew the speed of the current I'd make a calculation. You can learn how to do these things from a Jules Verne book, too bad I don't have one of those on board. It never interested old Homer to divulge technical details while telling the tribulations of Ulysses, although a ten-year voyage would not exactly be the ideal situation in which to learn the navigational arts...It's getting cold. Irritated by hours of sun, my body suffers as the temperature drops. The salt makes my hands and feet swell up, my spine hurts. I need to stretch, walk around, move my muscles, or else manage to fall asleep. If it weren't for the physical discomfort, what I'm seeing might seem phantasmagorical: the silhouette of a man who converses in an unmelodious voice about sailing and bravery, among shadows which repeat the serenade of docks and beaches in the form of waves. The moon white, chilly, round, poetic, and in love with a summer that's the same as twenty others poorly spent on land. What I'm seeing is what's real, and I'm having trouble understanding that. Misery is simple, not mysterious, no different from what I know; sunburn is sunburn, cold is cold, and pain is pain. It's me who can't quite situate myself in this dark and unpredictable Gulf that speaks to me in a language that my remotest ancestor once knew.

It would be strange and illogical if my senses found this language coherent. I've got the disease of "naturalism," or what happens when somebody who's used to buildings and sirens and barking dogs finds himself in surroundings that I've decided to call "uterine," that is, places as devoid of the emblems of modernity as those of two thousand years ago. There's you and nature, or, better, there's you inserted into nature, rather than nature inserted in you. You've returned to the uterus you left fifty centuries back. So your perceptions return to their origins, and your terror is not that of the integrated circuit era, but that of the barbarians who painted buffalo on the walls of caverns so as to hunt them in their dreams. Here, I realize the enormous dependence of human beings on their history. It's not only that what is natural exists without relation to consciousness; if human beings didn't have on hand the privileges of consciousness—derived from their past—they'd lose themselves in the face of the sovereignty of what has been here forever. The old heroes are stuck inside the yellowed pages of their chroniclers, while those of today lie robbed of their power by technology and politics decreed from the inside of a Mercedes. History didn't end when the Berlin Wall fell; James Watt killed history with his steam engine. What remains, for us, is a fabulous incapacity to confront the world without a motor. Aboard

The Social Contract, I've got nothing to confront it with except my head and that of the Commodore, two thinking phenomena awaiting a verdict on our prohibited incursion. Although barbarian fear stalks us, we possess the consciousness of the present, which strips us of the fighting instinct that the inhabitants of the uterus had. We'll have to appeal to what the perfectionists of our system taught us, but there the combat is only between humans and ideas, never solitude or helplessness or the psychoses provoked by the medium you thought you controlled. I maintain that all members of society should submit themselves to a uterine test. It would be the graduation diploma that authorized their collective coexistence.

I'm listening to the Commodore because he deserves it. If Robinson Crusoe spent twenty-eight happy years in the company of a senile parrot and a trained native, why do I insist on isolating myself from someone on the basis of very civilized differences? He likes Whitney Houston and I like Frank Zappa; he likes busty women and I can't abide them. In spite of this, I accept a brotherhood that gives us relief from internal monologue. Certainly, destiny doesn't care about our personalities. What is written will happen, and my love of art won't save me, nor will his masculine autocracy save him. So, curious, I ask him to tell me something about his years as a military man. I'll begin to learn about the ups and downs of a sailor in times of revolution. The Commodore has travelled the coast of our island from end to end. He knows its paradises—the southern archipelago, or the northern shore of Camagüey with its eighty thousand flamingos. He's tasted the exquisite meat of the iguana, fillets of sea tortoise and twenty-inch snappers stuffed with purple onions and wild garlic grilled over charcoal made from the hardwoods of the swamps. Hundreds of times he's stood guard in the keys, surrounded by tall mangroves that vomit forth hordes of mosquitoes that can't be driven off by the smoke of burning dung or by waving palm leaves. Their sharp spikes pierce the cotton uniforms, their whine destroys the ears, they penetrate the defenses of innocent victims until they die in tiny explosions of blood when the desperate soldier crushes them. They never abandon their positions without refilling their bellies with the vital purple, leaving the skin splattered with pustules and lumps. He spent long months with the taste of salt on his lips, and his skin hardened by the sea-spray. Then would come days of shore leave, of drunken sprees and trampy girls, because in a country without whores in its ports there's no way to satisfy the implacability of desire except with the female friends of friends, who occasionally slip into movie theaters to see the Russian version of Pinocchio and secretly show off their own master-prints of oral sex. "The service sucks," the Commodore tells me while scratching his neck, and I believe him. There are plenty who get lucky and don't have such a hard time, but that wasn't his luck. What's curious is that I never heard him boast before about that tough life. No, he's not a braggart. His profile may be narrow, but he has the soul of a true *gallego*[8]: resignation toward life's ingratitudes, capacity to put up with a lot, and the zeal to find the land of milk and honey that Jehovah promised to the Israelites. Although, on the outside he pretends to be a card-carrying member of the "Macho-Me" club, and says that happiness is just pussy with beer.

---

[8] *gallego*: Galician, an immigrant from the Spanish province of Galicia, but popularly and somewhat pejoratively used to refer to Spaniards in general.

MILE 26

Before sleep, we throw dice. We bet a finger of water per throw, but after losing half a cup I decide to quit. The Commodore goes to sleep early, and I'm here counting stars, as they say. It would be great if it could all end tomorrow. Things ought to end when they start to get to you. Or so I think, in pursuit of my triumphalist longings. There are memories that can be enjoyed forever in spite of not having been lived, once the good times start to roll. Therefore it's better to anticipate your future pleasures and right away start creating the details which later, when you evoke them, will make you happy. For example, if tomorrow night I were to be sleeping peacefully in a room, safe and sound, I would think about myself as I am now, bathed in insecurity, and this would carry with it a delicious joy. Now, I have to distract myself from despair by thinking of tomorrow's happiness.

I want to sleep and empty my head of evasions. I'm going to count stars: one, two, three, four, five, six, seven, eight, nine, ten...this is no good. Maybe it would be better to self-induce catalepsy of the eyelids, the way they do in hypnosis. They say that with intelligent people, it can't fail. Let's see. I need to sleep, eleven; I need to sleep, twelve; I need to sleep, thirteen; I need to sleep, fourteen; I need to sleep, fifteen; I need to sleep, sixteen; I'm sleepy, seventeen; I'm very sleepy, eighteen; very sleepy, nineteen; my eyelids are heavy, twenty; my eyelids are heavy, twenty-one; very heavy, twenty-two; I can't lift them, twenty-three; impossible to lift,...I'm asleep, twenty-four; I'm deeply asleep, twenty-nine; I'm sleeping..., thirty; I'm sleeping, thirty-one...

THIRD DAY
8:31 A.M.

MILE 31

The Commodore is in heaven because he caught a three-pound pompano. He says he's going to cook it the same way Gregorio does, the owner of the famous Pilar where Hemingway carried on his Caribbean adventures. Fish in general doesn't do much for me, but I can see that this one looks really good. Scaled and cleaned, it is an offering of tempting white flesh that the Commodore smears with lemon and then hands me on a stick. "Fried with butter, it's worth your life," he affirms euphorically. An acquaintance with the deeds of the Nobel prize winner is almost obligatory among men of the sea; if he never read any of his books, at least he respectfully remembers the Stockholm medal that Hemingway donated to the Virgin of the Caridad de Cobre in Santiago de Cuba, a stroke which won him the approval of the Catholics and quite a few prayers for the peace of his soul. What's for sure is that the fish tastes good. It's a splendid lunch which gives us an excuse to talk for a long while about maritime cuisine. Historically, my preferences tend toward lobster and emperor crab. The Commodore bursts out laughing, saying this is the typical taste of those who miss the essence of the white meats of fish. Suddenly he's excited, telling me about I-don't-know-how-many species, which reminds me of the famous dialogue between Captain Nemo and Professor Aronnax, where the former explains at great length the variety of an oceanic menu, including portentous marine beasts whose flavor mimics the perfection of beef and pork. And I go on thinking about this without paying much attention to the enthusiastic speech of my comrade, now involved in exalting a certain type of red crayfish which constituted the ultimate delicacy for the Taino shamans of Baracoa five hundred years ago.

This afternoon it's my turn to try fishing. With the straw hat protecting my head from the sun, I kneel in the prow waiting for a fish. A fish that never appears, and convinces me I wasn't born with a talent for this job. Only once in my life did I succeed in catching a fish. It happened on a river bank, and it made me so happy that afterward I spent entire weeks in pursuit of that special moment when you feel the spasms of the fish you tricked transmitted back along the line.

Now I don't have the patience for it. My face is stinging and my skull is sweating buckets under the hat; I'd rather rest a while. I hand the rod over to the Commodore and go back to my books. But this is no moment for reading; since morning I've begun to note the first symptoms of the tedium that surrounds me. What was curious or interesting yesterday, today I find bothersome. The signs of physical degradation—still faint— grow closer. My skin stings, and it's turning slowly from an epithelial red to a funereal bronze that extends over my face, neck, and hands, redoubts undefended by the thick uniform I wear. But the worst—and I should have guessed this—is the invariability of the panorama. The

crushing presence of the blue-sky-sea robs me of my
reflective inspirations and demands that I reckon with it
directly, which I fear will very soon be difficult to
evade...The day goes by more slowly. This is to be expected because that's what happens when routine
achieves a monopoly, and it worsens over time. I sleep
in snatches, read short stories from *One Thousand and
One Nights*, watch the gulls, and watch the clouds that
fly over us like cotton giants, like winged clipper ships
carrying shadows along. I think and think and think. Finally, after a late nap, it gets dark again. Conversation
time, the ceremony that comes before sleep. It's my turn,
and without much preamble I begin describing a dissi-
pated life in which the extravagant clashes with the alarm-
ingly moderate: I paint. I explain that not all painters are
the same. I don't go around in threadbare clothes nor cut
my hair short nor leave it long. I am no aficionado of
those bohemian bars that spring up in the city every fifteen days. I don't think of myself as apolitical, which I
see as a hypocritical ideology, a last refuge of soldier
boys turned spiteful by the eternal contradictions. I prefer to tell my companion—without the slightest fear of
being misunderstood, even knowing his limitations—two
or three of my desires, pleasant and original ones, nothing more. For example, I'd like to paint a twenty by five
meter mural that tells the history of the Indian Hatuey.
In it, next to the stake where the supposed heretic burns,
I show a whole Parnassus stuffed full of apostates condemned by the Roman Catholic Church in its thousand
years of papal absolutism. Another very attractive idea,
I'd also like to visit the great shrines of art: the Louvre,
the Sistine Chapel, the Prado, the Hermitage, the Pyramids. But if I started to explain to the Commodore the
why and wherefore of each of these, we'd be at it till
morning. He knows this and so doesn't ask. He opts for
saying, sadly, "That's a whole world, all right." Although
he doesn't know Michelangelo or Botticelli, he recog-

nizes the grandeur of the patrimony that must exist out there, from which he jumps to the supposed disgrace of my having lived twenty years without real access to this mirage. It's as if someone like him living in Denmark were bemoaning the lack of a partner to dance *casino* with. "Cuba would have gone far if it hadn't been for the Revolution. We'd be the South Korea of the Americas, and home to the best Latino painters," he says in an attempt to console me. He doesn't know a damn thing about it. For a while now I've been convinced that my sister's boyfriend is passing through a stage in which his disdain for communism is making him into the Judas of his own harmony, but I let him please himself with his irrefutable proof, which lies in the stories about his grandparents' prosperity in the time of Grau San Martín.[9] He says they were coffee processors who owned I-don't-know-how-many Cadillacs. Maybe it's true, but I part company with those who lament the lost glitz and glitter, or invent a false grandeur for the banana republic, or remain a bunch of hypocrites after thirty years of celebrating the Twenty-Sixth of July with roast pork and marching to the plaza for Party events. The Commodore is a right-wing nostalgic whose knowledge of Marxism consists of the tidbits he memorized on the night before an exam: that the basis of exploitation is surplus value and its discoverer was the guy with the long hair and bushy beard whose portrait is the constant-pi of our schoolbooks (most people don't know about his Jewish heritage or his Cuban son-in-law). When they think about the term *WORKER,* they imagine a turn-of-the-century factory bursting with ragged souls demanding a wage increase, which they think is quite different from the working class hero formed in the Saxon tradition. "Times have changed," we are assured by those who deem the era of *Les Miserables* over. Today's employee buys this

---

[9] Dr. Ramón Grau San Martín: elected president in 1944 on the basis of his reputation as a reformer, but thereafter known chiefly for the corruption of his administration.

year's Mazda—designed for him—in monthly payments, and goes off in his Bermuda shorts to sip piña coladas in Martinique. And I laugh, hearing an argument that I used to hear only from the surfers of Santa María beach, the disco boys, and the pimps who drive Havanautos jeeps and screw in the bungalows of Gran Caribe tourist hotels.[10] But suddenly, I cut off this pretentious painter, myself, in the process of explaining to his sister's man that the one who reigns in the North is the son-of-a-bitch with the loudest hype, and simply detesting the Marxist classics won't guarantee you rent for an apartment every month. The truth is, I'd be delighted and I'd find it fitting to arrive at New York's Museum of Modern Art and Venice's Bienalle with my "indigenist" canvasses under my arm, wild to win the favor of the critics. Nonetheless, I fear that path as much as I do the one on which I'm now risking my neck. This has its good points and its bad ones. Distrust of the prize helps you bear failure, and at the same time denies you the ability to go all out, which is sometimes the only way to achieve your ends. The Commodore says I am complicating my life. "I sure hope so," I reply, very sure of the contrary. Our different opinions take shelter behind an army of "I-sure-hope-so's." I, at least, confer a great portion of my scruples onto him, I protect myself from maintaining any illusions, while he charges directly toward a Byzantine pseudo-glory in which he will later take his own dreams to task as he watches stagecraft angels fall.

[10] Havanautos and Gran Caribe: state corporations selling services to foreign tourists.

FOURTH DAY

MILE 39

Today when I got up I noticed my bodily ills more than ever. In spite of the sunscreen, the exposed areas of my flesh look as if the skin had been replaced with old Scotch tape. A lingering vapor steams from my pores, dampening my clothes. I feel as if my flesh were full of sand and all I want to think about is a stream of fresh, cold, transparent, bubbling water falling over me and driving my lethargy away. For breakfast, I drink a glass of chocolate milk. We ought to catch another pompano to get a break from these cans, because I've had it with the ham. Luckily, the Commodore proclaims good news: we're having hot dogs for lunch. It's meat just the same, but out here the slightest difference in taste is cause for rejoicing in my stomach...This morning I notice some larger fish around the raft. The Commodore thinks they're shad, and his judgment is confirmed when he sees them jump out of the waves, showing us their long greenish dorsal fins. "They're no good to eat," he tells me, while they vanish from our sight, heading south. We are also visited by dark, undefinable shadows in the blue. They limit themselves to passing under *The Social Contract* like tortured souls avoiding contact, but their presence as amorphous enigmas is enough. It's strange that so far no sharks have appeared. They're capable of spotting irregular motion in the water from far off. These rafts are designed to float on the ocean's surface as inconspicuously as possible, but that's no guarantee against the formidable detection capabilities of a shark. And we've still got a number of days left to test that out... The more we enter into this static universe inhabited by fear and beauty, the less I understand those who underestimate the power of the sea. It's incredible that some people can throw themselves into the Gulf, totally alone, atop an inner tube with a ridiculous supply of two bottles of water and a bag of bread. That's not bravery, and it's not desperation. It's just being a stupid asshole—the kind who, if he manages to survive, has the right to blow his life's salary in a casino because he's such a lucky guy. I'm congratulating myself for the luck of the past few days, though I know the worst is still to come. To outwit the physical drain we a have very simple strategy: take sleeping pills. We've got some packets of nitrazepam on board that will keep us asleep most of the time. It's like the kind of hibernation proposed by the people who dream up voyages into hyperspace. We share their conclusion about the impossibility of staying alert in noxious conditions. This way we can immunize ourselves against cabin fever and its deceits.

MILE 43

The best thing about lunch was the juice the hot dogs came in. Imagine, in Cuba I was disgusted just touching the stuff. Here, we split it evenly and, given the conditions, it provided an unexpected relief. After we ate, the Commodore calculated our position and told me, worried, that we keep drifting too far to the west, into the Gulf of Mexico. "We're going to have to take turns rowing to correct our course," he announced. The idea didn't do much for me. I don't feel destroyed by the days of exposure to the sun, but just thinking of making any physical effort gives me cramps. I don't know if I've got the strength, but I decide to accept on the condition that we'll only row at night...Leaning back against the bow, I try to read a pamphlet on Buddhism, but on the first page I get hit with a bad headache followed by a cold sweat. I close my eyes and lean forward, head down and hands pressing my temples until the throbbing slowly starts to disappear, after which I'll stay in that position a long time, fearful that the symptoms will return. Clearly my periods of literary evasion are done with. This has been a signal from my body, a warning of what's ahead. My mind can't handle the intellectual drain of reading anymore. Extraordinary evidence that the damage is internal as well. Up to now it's been an external ordeal—damaged skin, burning or cold—but now nature is putting a new strategy into effect, one that consists of provoking a terrible dementia capable of undermining my survival instinct step by step. And who could be less well-prepared for this than myself, the hapless painter? A few furious attacks and I'll be reduced to one of those walking crazies you see on the street. I can feel my fear again in a fluttering heartbeat, and this time I don't doubt it. In spite of the Commodore's protests I swallow the first nitrazepam.

"I'm not going to allow a single neuron to get fucked up," I answer back to him before stretching out face down on the gritty floor of the raft to await the effect. I entertain myself with the heavy-eyelid counting, although I don't get past twenty this time.

MILE 46

I wake up after six in the evening, just in time to observe the first shark of the voyage, visible as a prototypical dorsal fin cutting through the waves about fifty meters away. "Should have seen them earlier," mused the Commodore with an old sea-dog's patience. The beast came directly toward the raft, then dove just half a meter before it would have hit us. I realized I'd stopped breathing and my muscles had tensed up as if resisting a ton of iron. The shark reappeared on the port side, displaying most of its gray back. "Less than a meter long," my comrade assures me as if this signified that it's toothless and doesn't like meat. The only words I manage are, "It's horrible," twice. Before the shark repeats the maneuver, the Commodore pulls two bottles of fuel oil from one of the knapsacks and starts to spill its contents around *The Social Contract*. I don't think this will do much damage to the damned thing, and neither does my comrade, but there's nothing to lose by trying—even though we know that if the shark is really hungry, there's no stopping it.

The shark completed a parabola and turned toward us again. I armed myself with a precious diver's knife and waited with my knees balanced on the side of the raft, ready to plunge the knife with the most force I could muster. The Commodore perched in the same position on the starboard side to maintain the boat's equilibrium, brandishing a bayonet. The oil floated by me in the form of successive shiny streaks, moving off with the current. When the shark was three or four meters from the boat, its fin sank under the water and I could see its shadow go by, a mere thirty centimeters below my post. I could even see the convoy of pilot fish that swam alongside it. I shouted to the Commodore that we had it underneath us. With my free hand I grabbed one of the hand-holds along the side of the boat and waited for the shock of contact. But the shark surfaced more than fifteen meters away. Apparently the dispersed oil must have bothered it, and it preferred to go deeper rather than attack something as bad tasting as that. It kept its distance for quite a while, not trying to approach again. I passed some time reflecting on how different it is to see animals in the placidity of aquariums, bored in their glass cells, foolish, inoffensive, and incapable of scaring even little girls. This one, on the other hand, captivated me. To see it in its true medium—and considering my situation—it's enough to make you pray. The feared fish, the legendary man-eater distorted (but how much?) by the Spielbergian fantasy. Solemn and discreet, it seems to be asking, "Didn't you want to get to know me?" My comrade smiles at seeing me so affected. I say, "I can't believe it's for real," but he answers with a cluck of disagreement.

"You ain't seen nothing yet," he tells me. "What you've got there is just a pup. What's really something is when you run into a tiger shark or a hammerhead fighting for a piece of meat. They go crazy. They do circles and circles around the carcass blinded by the smell, and suddenly they lunge, and there's no way in hell to stop them. If they're travelling in packs, they can dismember each other too."

I ask him if there isn't any danger of them taking bites out of our raft. I've heard since childhood that red attracts sharks. He thinks not, as long as we don't run into the ones he just described, in which case we wouldn't be safe even in a wooden boat. Luckily, the one we saw was travelling alone, or perhaps it was a scout sent out to survey the terrain. The Commodore has a .38 revolver stashed in the pocket of his camouflage, but this could just make matters worse; a bloody mess around us could mean the end of *The Social Contract*...and the end of our voyage too. Of course, they aren't really like the ones in American movies: murderers of anything that moves in the sea. Quite likely they could consider us a trifling thing and forget about the raft. My sister's boyfriend shakes his head in clear negation. "Better ask God to keep them far away, in the Gulf there's no mercy for anything. Here the sharks even eat the cans thrown overboard from yachts. We're a hell of a feast, compared to that."

I spent the rest of the afternoon scanning the sea from horizon to horizon. When I have to toss any garbage overboard, I throw it so far that there can't be any trail leading from it to us. How fucked up, how completely fucked up it is to be in my place.

MILE 47

A mist has started to spread along the horizon; a graying stripe that clashes with the late afternoon phosphorescence of the sea. I'd rather it were a mirage than the arrival of bad weather or heavy seas. Even with all the damage the sun does, it's better to see it, torrid and irritating, since it offers us the peacefulness of a docile sea. I can just imagine a hurricane this far out; the waves towering ten meters above us, dancing *The Social Contract* on their peaks, then plunging us into a labyrinth of tunnels below. From my adolescent memory appear the shipwrecked legends who overcame the worst typhoons of literature: Robinson Crusoe, founder of the Western race of castaways, the sailors of the *Liguria*, Sinbad, the prophet Jonah too. All of them are dancing a dance of ill-omen around the raft, a rite in honor of Poseidon, king of the whirlpool and the trident. The difference is that in their literary incarnations, none of them perished. Quite the contrary, they took advantage of their tragedies to arrive at a paradise of white isles overflowing with parrots and colors. I don't have this option, even if the benefits of Eden are attributed to certain coasts. I'd happily give ten years of my life to do without an angry sea. The Commodore calms me down, alleging that this is an unimportant phenomenon of the climate. "If you don't feel a change in the air, don't go suffering just for the fun of it," he explains. We should go on trusting in our lucky star. The visibility is perfect, and the proper thing to do is breathe in the peace and silence. But supposing that I'm practically arriving at my destination—assuming the U.S. Coast Guard does its job—I'd really be disgusted if the whole thing went to the dogs thanks to a meteorological disturbance that wiped me off the map without anyone knowing, unless my body washed up against the houses of a happy village somewhere. The wise meteorologists would grant this disturbance a place in their ranking of disasters, conferring upon it a sensual and attractive woman's name.

The nitrazepam pill left me ravenous. I ate two rolls with hot dogs, and half a can of pears. Afterward, to air out my body, I took off the camouflage shirt I've worn since the day before yesterday and let the northerly breezes caress my flesh before wrapping myself in a cotton sheet which feels glorious after the rough cloth of the uniform. I have to wear that odious shirt to prevent the sun from opening up more holes in my hide. It's terrible to feel this stifling heat, the vapor emanating from your skin, while your head is a fireball and you don't know if it's better to take your hat off or leave it on. My ideas evaporate, while the shining rebounds from the waves onto each of my cheeks and sets them aflame. At night I can think about this, taking advantage of the nocturnal cold that has made it bearable. By day, I prefer to fix my vision on a single point and give free rein to dreams of escape...I don't know why I should be worrying. Yes, of course I know: the fuel light is winking because my tank is getting closer and closer to empty every minute that goes by...I'll spend most of tomorrow asleep, except for breakfast, lunch, and dinner. I don't know how bad this is for me really, because there aren't any sedatives without side effects, but I can't do anything else—or, better, I don't want to.

MILE 49

The Commodore has asked me to take the oars to fulfill what we settled over lunch. It will be our first argument of the trip because I'm forced to tell him that I can't do what we agreed. I feel very weak. He's half-enraged and repeats that I have to take the oars. I refuse again. "You're a yellow faggot who only knows how to hold paintbrushes and chicken feathers," he says, throwing his hat at me. I block it with a wave of my hand, which sends it into the water. "Get it back," he says with a stupid look in his eyes. I glance at the sea and realize that the hat has already been carried too far by the waves. Trying to avoid the fight that's coming, I tell him its dangerous to swim so far, but if he wants my hat I'll give it to him. What do I care about honor with this ball of muscle facing me and all the odds on his side? "I want my hat," he declares. This is getting ugly. Patience, patience, I shouldn't react too fast. If I provoke him, I'm lost. I direct my attention to the water again, but now there's nothing to be seen, it's all been swallowed up by the night. "It's been swallowed up by the night," I say. "Even if they wanted to, nobody could find it now."

"My hat, you're going to bring me my hat or I'll throw you in," the Commodore persists. Immediately I respond, "Uh-huh, and when you get to Miami what the hell will you tell my sister? She won't ever forgive you even if it's not your fault, you can forget the good life, they'll jail you as a drug addict and when..."

In one leap he's on top of me, his hands are closing around my neck while he repeats, "You piece of shit, you piece of shit." I hit him in the ribs with the energy of someone fighting for his life, but it doesn't get me anywhere. I'm losing air. I try to breathe, but the oxygen can't get through my throat. The Commodore's thick fingers tighten and tighten on my windpipe; I open my mouth like a fish and feel my head fogging over...my life is going...Suddenly the pressure is gone and I'm coughing with my eyes full of tears, taking deep breaths, my heart beating wildly...After some time, calmer, I see the Commodore lying in the stern with his eyes vacant, distinguishable by the light of a lantern he's lit for some reason. Seeing me, he turns it off. "Angel," I call out in a voice I don't recognize, "aren't we falling into despair?" He doesn't answer. Instead he says, "I hope no one finds us."

I wake up a little before midnight. Rapid heartbeats woke me, maybe a nightmare that seized its chance and then disappeared. The moon's great white ball shines on a tame sea and the face of the Commodore, who is sleeping like a log among the knapsacks. At this hour my friends must be in Roxana's house, loosest of the loose. Today is her birthday and they've got plans for a big bash, which equals no less than five bottles of rum and other details. She may have been the only one who sniffed out the possibility of my departure. Two or three days before I left, she asked me if I would give her my Jim Morrison book. I gave it to her with my best smile. Poor thing, she's been infected by that guy's personality. She knows the words to his songs, memorizes his poems, and has a collage of his photos decorating the longest wall of her room. Maybe my present will make her think of me today. She'll say, "Where in hell is that bad seed of a guy?" That's how she talks; things are good seed and bad seed, and that's how she stands out from people who use ordinary slang. I'll send her a cassette with my voice dubbed over the Doors' song "The End." And I'll give her a pile of some erotic stuff so she can get goosebumps all over and remember the good times we spent in her room, where she made me the stud of her unbridled whims. It happened inside a circle of candles, while she spoke to me in a South American accent about the joys of Tantra and the morals of Boccaccio. And yet this loser of a Commodore thinks that painting is just for queers. I've rarely seen anybody go after it like these imitators of Frida Kahlo. Their drive toward moral liberation is outside the logic of morals. The phallus-god, the cult of the vagina, exorcising the last spiteful remnants of Spanish puritanism. From brush-stroke to brush-stroke, from poem to poem, they rush to make literary confessions with the seal of the "Vertical Smile," they fondle sitars inside a cloud of incense, they fornicate with little contained cries of whores, and in their canvasses they ejaculate perpetual summits with symbols of pyramids. It was a historic misfortune when art opted for emancipation early in this century. The artists sat in the cafes proclaiming the secrets of Dr. Freud's couch, they wrote spicy elegies, and they enlisted in the Left to bring an end to the demagogy of the dressing room. When the October Revolution triumphed, they thought the Phariseeism of the bourgeois morality was gone; good-bye marriage and parasitic institutions. But the anarchy of the senses, the empire of free thought, all of that sank as soon as it became clear that the plebeians suffered from sanctimonious prudery just as much as the lords. In Cuba—perhaps owing to the question of hot tropical blood—feminism adopted the emblem of a rifle and learned to give birth according to European standards. But liberated sexuality—I'm referring more to lewd fascinations than to social rights—continued to be a privilege of artists. Therefore Roxana makes love only with creators: painters, poets, dramatists, sculptors, musicians, puppeteers, and videographers. From each one she demands an imaginative contribution that will match her own. She's interested in comparison for the sake of assessing talent—which in turn she can feed back into the passion of her brush. Tonight she'll sleep with one of them. She'll be frolicking in her bed on the floor until five in the morning, and then she'll consult the I Ching and assure her lover that this copulation was foreseen on the faces of the coins. This is Roxana, the super-trashy, the first person from my country whom I miss...I don't think that sleep will put in a return appearance just to make me happy. I search in one of the knapsacks for the packet of nitrazepam and only manage to wake up the Commodore. Of course his first words were curses, remnants of his anger about the rowing. So as not to waste time, I explain my plan to take a sedative, and he loses his temper even more. "You're like an old fucking maid swallowing all those pills!" he yells at me with his tongue half-tied. I stand firm in my decision not to argue; I tell him to go to hell and light the lamp to go on looking for those wonderful pills. When I've finally got them, I hear him saying, more calmly now, "I think it would be better for you to stay up talking with me, and save your sleepiness for when the sun is out."

That's not a bad idea, curiously I hadn't hit on the notion of reversing the normal schedule. If we give up sleeping at night we'll be more open to the effect of the sleeping pills during the hours of "truth." Okay, I say, what are we going to talk about? "About whatever," says the Commodore, "Let's see, why don't you tell me about some book, one of those you're reading?" Not a bad idea either. I know a ton of people who can find the oral version of *Don Quixote de la Mancha* or one of Shakespeare's works marvelous; they just can't subject themselves to the authors' linguistic whims. The best thing about those versions is the magic they work on the original stories, converting them into the most sympathetic and pleasant, or the most horrifying and captivating. Nonetheless trying to think of a book that will catch the attention of my comrade, I'm inclined to turn to Verne. So I appeal to his own judgment. "Tell me which you'd like to hear," I ask as if I were an aged storyteller. "The Bible," he replies almost immediately. "Won't that keep you talking till dawn?" Great joke, we could be talking about the Bible for four months without even getting to the New Testament.

"So, tell me the story of Jesus Christ," he asks, surely thinking of the painting of the Sacred Heart of Jesus which presided over the living room of his childhood home. It happened that way for all of us. We learned to look at it suspiciously because in school they didn't want to reveal the secret to us, while He continued to be a mystery beloved by the widows of the neighborhood. It's a myth I enjoy telling, and this isn't the first time. So, after an inspiring pause I bring my sister's boyfriend up to date on the son of Mary and Joseph, the one conceived without sin, who today rules over a billion souls. It's difficult, really, to understand the reason for his proscription on our island. The Commodore doesn't think much about this; in his opinion it's one more item in evidence of communist despotism, but the thing is not so simple, I explain. The Church—this institution more powerful than marriage and the state of law—tends to be controversial. Today it may save lepers, while yesterday it burned scholars. The hammer and sickle dared to challenge it, promulgating an Eden achievable on earth, called communism, which neither angels nor devils could enter within. The only ones admitted would be those who reserved their tickets through the class struggle. Then some Pope had an image of the Vatican converted into a museum and the Chair of St. Peter into a postcard, and so he screamed "Sacrilege!" and swore to make war on these new thieves of consciousness. Logically, both sides have the complete right to defend their roads to paradise, even if (as the Commodore well knows) the version minus angels is not in vogue right now. What does bother me, and this is what I keep quiet about, is the current revival of believers who have no idea where they are going to end up taking shelter. The majority of them

don't know beans about God but applaud his commandments for their attractive quality of denying the fundamental problem of being and consciousness. These are
the same ones who, three decades ago, took down the
Sacred Heart and replaced it with a photo of Fidel.

The Nazarene is a thorny subject, just like
his crown. Dawn will come and catch us still arguing
over the veracity of his miracles. And that argument opens
the doors to others whom no one invited: the court of the
Orishas, African saints, deities, and spirits. The Commodore begins speaking of incarnations and the dead;
and what about Babalú Ayé, and what about Changó,
and what about Elegguá, and what about evil influences
and spells and ghosts? At this moment he remembers all
the souls hurt by his actions—or not. "I'm sure something exists," he says in a pathetic tone, "I don't know
whether it's God or a Mandinga devil but something is
up there, and we need to show it respect."

Now I'm almost getting scared. In the
middle of the darkness which still surrounds us, these
macabre subjects can make me see demons where there's
nothing but a darkened sea. If I tell him to change the
subject he'll realize this, and then the time will go by in
a shittier way than it already has. So I decide to take the
initiative: "In your ship, didn't they tell you the story of
the sailors who disappeared in the Bermuda Triangle?"
Obviously he hasn't heard about this, he'll ask me to tell
him and I'll do it, showing off my marvelous capacity
for narrating fatal events, recreating my worst fears of
these four days with a sickening sadism that frightens
me. Luckily the sun rises and I stop talking. It's time to
sleep. It's time to disconnect from all of this, because I
begin to suspect that I'm going nuts.

FIFTH DAY
8:45 A.M.

MILE 53

At daybreak, to battle stations. The Commodore shook me awake with the news of a ship in sight. Rubbing my eyes and looking in the direction indicated by his arm, I can make out in the distance a silhouette of considerable size. I'm about to explode with joy, assuming the best, when I hear him say: "It's a Cuban navy patrol boat, I know that silhouette as well as my mother's." He explains that they are rarely seen so many miles from the coast, and usually do not busy themselves with rafters, but it's better for us to avoid being seen. We'll try to get out of their field of vision; I stretch out in the bottom of the raft, and he takes charge of the oars. With caution, we begin to move. My comrade gives himself over to an effort that's exhausting after a hundred hours adrift. From my post I can feel his breathing, which intensifies as the oars take bigger bites out of the sea. Forward and back, forward and back, his muscles contract again and again, sweat bathes his skin and a whistle emerges from his lungs. I poke my head over the edge and see the ship much closer, really it doesn't seem like a military craft, I can't make out any guns on the deck, to me it looks more like a deep-drawing yacht. I don't know whether they've seen us, but they sure are narrowing the gap. I know it and so does the Commodore, who suddenly, without stopping his rowing, exclaims, "Pitch out the knapsack with your books." I freeze, but not because I want to refuse to do what he asks. It's a case of involuntary reaction in the face of losing my most precious cargo. He feels my confusion and turns toward me brusquely: "Didn't you hear? Throw them overboard. Shit, man. Throw 'em." I'm in torment on one side of the goddamn boat and on the other there's my sister's hysterical boyfriend incessantly ordering me to throw them, throw them, throw them out. I take the knapsack, raise it above me, and hurl it into the water. There it falls with a spectacular splash, stays afloat for a few seconds, and then disappears forever into the dark blue. I just hope we don't have to get rid of another one, or we might as well let ourselves be boarded. The Colossus continues rowing, more and more frenetically, desperately, maddened by the imperious urge not to fail. There are violent thrusts impelling *The Social Contract* now. He's terribly frightened. He knows he faces three or four months in prison for having stolen a life raft from an Armed Forces warehouse, and the pistol too; well, he can pitch that into the sea if there's no other way out. For me, on the other hand, it's thirty days in the Villa Marista[11] and a warm welcome from the neighborhood on my return. I'm clean. I'll only have to put up with some officer's speech about what will happen if I try again and an interrogation which begins with a very complicated "Why?" I'll tell him: look, officer, the thing is that we painters can't be tied to any government, we're interna-

---

[11] Villa Marista: headquarters of state security forces, formerly the property of the Marist Order of the Catholic Church.

tional. No, that's a mistake. That's the same justification the Jehovah's Witnesses give for not saluting flags or singing patriotic hymns. Plus, it would hand them the next question on a silver platter: "So, you're denying your country, is that it?" Of course not! Listen, I'm no *gusano* who leaves the country to get his photo taken in the supermarket with fat, pink relatives that nobody remembers. Do you want me to be honest? The truth is that I've got no desire—and don't get insulted, officer—to waste my life in this Tower of Babel trying to reach heaven, a beautiful dream, marvelous, but I don't want to screw myself for something I'm never going to see. You only live once and you've got to be very careful when the time comes to choose your path. Sure, if everybody thought like me we'd still be walking around in loincloths. That's how it is. For the world to be a world, it takes all kinds. My thing is painting, and you know that the picture here isn't exactly pretty. I'm betting everything on my talent, I trust in it, and I can get to taste pleasures that are still unknown to me. I'm not such an idiot as to try out the role of the defrauded revolutionary, that this one betrayed that one and that one betrayed I don't know who; that doesn't fit me, nor am I going to go speak on chickenshit radio stations that would swindle their own mothers with a line about free Cuba, beautiful Cuba; not on my life would I give that pleasure to those sons-of-bitches who don't give a damn whether I paint canvasses or live under a bridge. What matters to me is that I don't reach forty saying to myself in the mirror, "You're a fuck-up, you never made the slightest attempt to be somebody." Of course, you could reproach me for not playing your card, but I haven't got the blood of a redeemer to straighten this country out and disregard the vultures who make war on whomever doesn't smell good to them. They can take their official forms and their rules and their little speeches, and stuff them. At least, over there, I can do without all that, and anybody who gets in my way won't do it disguised as a communist or call me the devil in the name of Martí. If I were Che, that would be different, but the slogan didn't stop being just a slogan[12] because I repeated it for nine years in the courtyards of schools. You don't build Che's with chants. Sure, I'd like to live in the long-sought oasis without lines or bureaucrats, but until then I'd prefer not to enroll in the experiment. I wish you all the best in the world. You're the lords of philanthropy, and that's all you've got left to help you put up with the garbage, both outside and inside the country, with your white-shirted bureaucrats who get fat off the "sacrifices of the Fatherland." You know what fascinates me about capitalism? It's been around long enough that you always know the name of the syndrome that's walloping you, and believe me, that's a great consolation. I swear it on my mother, officer.

These justifications keep on parading through my head while, with my eyes closed, I expect any minute to hear a stentorian military voice announcing that our little game is done. But what I hear is the Commodore's voice calling me. *The Social Contract* has stopped. I stand up to see the Commodore sprawled in the stern with his arms hanging in the water and his camouflage suit unbuttoned to his waist. His chest is soaked in sweat and his breathing disturbed, but the expression on his face is glad. "And the patrol?" I ask while looking around without seeing a sign. "Gone," he announces, almost in a sigh. "The fucking ship didn't see us, it kept on going." It's incredible, after that scare I don't know whether or not to laugh at all the defensive arguments with which I provisioned myself. That storm of pretexts engendered by our flight seems exaggerated and even melodramatic. Nonetheless, it's good for these things to happen. A sudden fright renews the energy worn away by the emptiness of the days. After consternation comes a renewed urge to do something to get the adventure over

[12] the slogan: "We will be like Che."

with, and with luck that impulse gets us through whatever anxiety remains. The Commodore, done in by the
kilometer and a half he rowed, asks me for a sip of water, and while I'm looking for it he assures me in the
most optimistic way that we don't have to worry about
seeing any more Cuban ships; the next craft, we can sa-
lute with "Vivas!" and hats in the air. But soon I discover—and I look and look again without wanting to
believe it—something that suddenly makes me shiver
inside. The knapsack that went overboard wasn't the one
with my books, but the one that held all the canteens for
the trip, more than fifteen liters. My stomach heaves,
my nerves tremble, and my blanching face speaks for
itself. My comrade asks what's going on. "What's going
on," I explain to him, "is that I've put my foot in it up to
my balls…I got confused and threw the pack with the
canteens into the sea." His reaction is what you'd expect
when someone receives a shattering, undeserved blow
that allows no appeal: eyes wide, mouth gaping, a tongue
that tries to make sounds but can't. I ask him not to get
furious at me, it won't fix anything, it's too late for insults even if I'm the only one for fifty miles around who
deserves them. It's useless, his recovered tongue is a vi-
tuperating machine. His face, deformed by the outburst,
reflects incredible fury. I am, among other things, an
asshole who can't understand the seriousness of what
I've done, an imbecile and a coward, especially the lat-
ter. He accuses me of having panicked and acted out of
stupidity, but later he's thinking more carefully and adds,
"Maybe you did it on purpose, out of your weakness for
those shitty books." I try to convince him otherwise. What
kind of mind could do such a thing? If he hadn't gotten
me agitated, we wouldn't be arguing now. "If you had
left the books behind, like I asked, we wouldn't be arguing now," he paraphrases. For myself, I still wonder
whether the so-called patrol boat might have been merely
a civilian yacht. But I don't say so, because he'll just

think it's a dumb excuse on my part. And he's got a point: it wasn't an innocent mistake. At the moment of choosing which knapsack, my subconscious betrayed me, my id made the decision, taking advantage of my distraction during our flight. Damn culture, damn years spent worshipping books and more books, teaching myself in an autodidactic passion that tried to compensate for impossible yearnings toward a universal philosophy—they had to pop up and take their bows when I least expected them, and they've condemned me. I'd like to be able to explain that to the Commodore, but he's not going to understand any of it. I hardly understand myself how anything within my body could do this to me, expose me to the risk of a slow death by dehydration unless we're rescued within a few hours at most. The neurons that live inside my head have spun things around a hundred and eighty degrees. We're in the middle of an ocean, a situation that doesn't permit such costly mistakes. The patrol boat, or whatever it was, has abandoned us to our fate. In our flight from it, we may have passed up our last chance. I want to avoid being a pessimist...someone will appear. And that's what's hard, precisely, to want to but not be able to, because my anxiety is immense and oppressive...I shouldn't obsess about this or I'll panic. My sister's boyfriend is lying down in the stern trying to block out his irritation and fear with impossible sleep. As much as I'd like to, I wouldn't be able to do it even with nitrazepam, unless I took an elephant's dose. Will it turn out that the Colossus had been wrong? He, who knows the sea so well and dreams about the silhouettes of ships, he'll never accept it. And rightly; to perish because of such an absurd mistake constitutes horrible evidence of the irrationality of chance. The big irony is, the crew members of that ship won't be aware of the danger into which they drove two people without pursuing them, without hunting them, without firing a lousy shot. Simply complying with routine duty or taking a vacation trip. Back in port, they'll lie down to sleep, exhausted, or go out to kill their hunger in some greasy spoon, or to the movies, or fornicate with their girlfriends or boy-friends, never knowing of our existence. They won't tell their friends (or, if they're soldiers, their superior) of any extraordinary event. Eleven million Cubans (my family among them), all oblivious to the agony about to over-take us. Sabina[13] had it right: destiny is a motherfucker.

[13] Joaquín Sabina: a Spanish singer and songwriter.

MILE 54

We haven't said a word in ten hours. And it's better this way, because I don't know any that would be appropriate for moments like these...

In only eight hours thirst has revealed its true self, in only eight hours, my God. For five days I could keep it within bounds, thinking I was getting used to managing it. But the sly son-of-a-bitch has just been hiding in a corner till now. Thirst is a mustard-colored cup with tiny cold droplets dribbling down its sides. It's already lodged itself into my gray matter, and now there's no driving it out. It's a virus...and the incubation period ended eight hours ago. Before that, the symptoms were ambiguous: headache, dryness in the throat, desire to drink; now the symptoms are broader, encompassing a variety of agonies. Thirst is not some idea I dreamed up, it's alive and can do perfectly well without my attention. It begins with a thickening of the saliva, minute by minute increasing in viscosity, concentrating into a heavy, compact mass that's hard to swallow, to say the least. On reaching the larynx it doesn't slide past, but adheres to the walls of the throat and slowly drips toward the stomach. And this slow dripping is maddening because what one wants is for this mass to finish sinking, one wants to feel some relief no matter how illusory and incapable of sustaining the organism. And you know this, and so begins the second phase: dry swallows. Up and down goes the Adam's apple, doing the impossible in order to transport what's left of water in this hot paste that travels between your teeth, the roof of your mouth, and your tongue. That little cup is growing in size and verisimilitude now. Its aluminum surface is more real, and you can almost feel the ice-cold drops. You close your eyes trying to reach it, and when you can't, you make the mistake of trying to think about something else, thereby becoming obsessed. For lack of water you resort to the breeze around you. You open your mouth and give the air entry into your lungs, trying to cool the inside of your body and the paste inside your throat. Now all the elements of torment are assembled, and they usher in the third stage in which each one lends itself to the cooperative task: the dense spittle stuck in your craw, the nonexistent cup always feeding your agony, and the hot air strangling you. Moment by moment more illusions appear, the *delirium tremens* of the seas. The yellow cup is the bearer of other aberrations; the object of an exhausting temptation that wants to settle accounts with the remnant of consciousness that's still loyal to me. To do so, the cup will have to bombard me with blows, sounds, the mirages of a dying man. Peeling loose, finger by finger, the hand with which I cling to what unfortunately is real. The cup will become a thousand cups and multiply my madness with vomit and cramps. I can picture the coming hell of my stomach enmeshed in tremendous pain.

MILE 55

We're not done for yet: we've found something to drink. It's not water—not the sweet, demanding, and potable substance of our sufferings—but it will do to extend our strength and sustain the hope that we could be protected by a guiding star. It was the Commodore's idea; he spent the afternoon sprawled in the stern attempting dry swallows and inhaling through his mouth—like me. Suddenly he got up, grabbed the knapsack of food, and pulled out everything: rolls, crackers, spam, sausages, and chocolate bars. When I saw him euphorically hold up a can of peaches, I understood what he'd been looking for. We opened it immediately, dividing the juice and pulp, a half cup for each. This was the only food of the day, because we had skipped lunch so as not to have to deal with dry mouthfuls. First the juice slid along my throat, moistening my larynx, and then the peach graced me with the sovereign pleasure of relief in my mouth. The liquid is too sweet, though, and won't hold off thirst for long. Meanwhile we took advantage of this consumption, swallowing two tablets of nitrazepam each which will have us sleeping like logs...As they take effect, I risk addressing my comrade, intrigued as I am by the disastrous destiny that awaits. I ask him how long he thinks we can last. The Commodore sucks the last swallow from his cup, throws the can into the sea, and answers without looking at me, "Not long." I want to know the extent of "not long." This time he clears up my doubts with slow words, premeditatedly sharp. "With sun like this, no more than two days." Nonetheless, that doesn't sound so fatal. Considering that today is the fifth one, this seems like a reasonable margin for being found. The hard part will be holding up until that second day. Before we were practically praying to get to the fifth, and now I'm begging heaven for two more, while the enormous gulf to the west is getting ready to swallow us up. It's as if we were inside a washroom sink, contemplating the whirlpool which spirals us closer to the drain at every turn...Here comes sleep, wrapping me in the same sheet as yesterday, and I feel a heavy weariness that dulls my muscles. Before I can escape, I discover the yellow cup in a corner of my thoughts, small and light but still present, hiding out in the nocturnal calm to surprise me tomorrow, my slave-driver once again.

SIXTH DAY

MILE 61

A horrible night. In my sleep, I hovered between a nightmare in which I starred as the thirsty protagonist and the fear that when I woke up it would be true—and it is. Even Jean Jacques Rousseau came to visit me with his wig and his speeches, infuriated that I'd plagiarized the name of his most illustrious work for an absurd and unjustifiable voyage. He went so far as to demand answers, as if I could clear up the great mystery of desperate souls. In the midst of thirst and delirium I tried to find the answers, but I could only think of doubt, of the situation of the Holy Trinity, and of the garbage which the modern humanistic tradition is...He wanted to discuss his discourse on the origin of inequality, to convince me I'd set off on an epic quest in search of the balance between society and nature...He spoke of destinations, my destination, which looks to be somewhere between cold mustard-colored deprivations, bad luck, and a far-off protest from my cheated proletarian roots.

Now I've woken up to the torment of the cup, pain in my guts, hunger, shakes, and saliva thicker than ever, with nausea as a preconscious state....Today I find the sound of the sea unbearable; it betrays some devious enemy setting traps. There's no more music in this repetition of sounds, this requiem that has replaced the poetic seashore melody, lovely for lovers and drunks and so intolerable for the dehydrated who've been listening for a hundred and twenty hours without a break...When the sun rises at last, the Commodore sits up. I don't think his night has been any better, maybe Rousseau didn't come to square accounts with him, but it could have been Our Lady of Miracles or some sailor friend who always had too much respect for the sea. What's for sure is that his eyes look desperate—as I'm sure mine do too—swollen and bloodshot. All of a sudden his tired voice starts telling me the story of a fisherman who survived twenty-one days at sea without a drop of water. To cope with his thirst he sucked the flesh of fish he caught and the blood of gulls that alighted on his boat to rest. "I didn't know gulls rested on boats," I tell him. His attempt to smile yields a caricature of happiness, and he adds, "I'll show you." Then he drew his revolver and, aiming carefully at a vague point in the sky, fired a shot. "Here comes one," he announced without changing his aim. Then another and another and another. At the fifth "gull," he broke out in hysterical laughter that fried my nerves. I feared he was going to take me for a giant bird or fish, just like what happened to Chaplin in that famous scene in *The Gold Rush*, but fortunately the Commodore recovered quickly, put the revolver away, and stared out to sea in a way that said nothing had happened at all. I relaxed, covered my face with the sheet, and tried to sleep although I knew it would take a major push. In the end, I don't know whether I made it or not. Between the heat, my craving for water, and my delirium, I must have gone through several periods of complete blackout, a type of amnesia that carried suffering to a different dimension. Coming back to reality, I found my comrade still observing the waters of the Gulf. "You're going to lose your sight expecting a miracle," I warned him, and he answered with great calm, "A storm's on the way." A day earlier I would have believed him, but not now. The sea exhibited no significant changes, and neither did the air. "Hallucinations," I thought, with my last gasp of hope.

MILE 62

I'm not going to pay any more attention to the cup. It stays in my head, looking for a way to drive me crazy. I'm not going to do a thing. I'll be present at the extinction of my body with the calm that a civilized person can manage. My cells are on strike, they refuse to accept the garbage I've given them, and none of them wants to work. As to my face, it's been skinned; when I pass my fingers along my cheeks and forehead I can feel the open sores of burned flesh. The slightest contact irritates them, lashing my nerves. To top off my maladies, I discover I can't see well. When I looked for the packet of nitrazepam, suddenly the images had ghosts like a television with the antenna out of whack. I rubbed my eyelids, opened and closed my eyes, but the effect didn't change. I now have to squint to make out anything small. This scares me plenty, indicating a deterioration that could be chronic, even in the event of a rescue. I hope it's nothing serious. The fact that it worries me means I haven't lost hope; it's better to trust in hope than in miracles. Nobody dies without trying everything....Jesus, do you hear me up there...? If only they'd taught me to pray...I only want you to help me...give me a few more days...I can't die, damn it..., twenty little years, just yesterday I was playing in the neighborhood without thinking life could be so hard, and it's so fucking hard...two more days. Look around me. Don't you see I'm alone among waves that buffet me around aimlessly? Don't you see this idiot at my side trying to kill me? And me, without any way to predict what he's going to do. If you're doing this on purpose, don't think I don't understand...there's a lot of shit in the world, but I've hardly lived..., you have to give me time, it's been only twenty puny years, at twenty you were a Joe Schmo carpenter. Who would've given a dime for you, huh? Excuse the irreverence, it's that I'm having so much trouble accepting what's happening to me..., think, Jesus, please, it's only been twenty little years...Hallowed be Thy name, God hold Thee and keep Thee in Glory..., lucky you, Jesus, it's not my fault. I swear I've never been anything but good, and the rest doesn't count because it's just the minimum done by anyone made of poor human blood...Are you going to let me die without doing anything? The worst is that it's so discouraging, to see myself done in by providence. If I can bear it, it's because I'm an intelligent person who doesn't let bad luck throw him. My fellow traveler, on the other hand, is in a giant crisis because he had Miami stuck in his head like a fucking photo and now he can't admit things turned out wrong. There's still time for you to help us, we're not bad people, we haven't believed in you because nobody bothered about that, but still, I read the Bible and I know about your anger and your kindness, please, don't let us die like this, in these hours of uncertainty we learned a lot, let us try it out. I won't promise you a hundred "Hail Mary's" or forty "Our Father's," nor that I'll crawl on my knees to every North American church begging people to pay tribute to you, but I'll show you that I'll go far, and when I get there I won't forget the God who saved my life at sea, like he saved Jonah before. That's what I'll promise you. Amen, amen, amen, amen, amen.

I'm taking more pills—a double dose— and I'm swallowing them broken into quarters because there's no liquid to carry them down. I gather up a great mouthful of frothy saliva and after a million tries I force the sedatives down at a snail's pace, leaving the bad chemical taste stranded in my throat. Then I cover my face with a t-shirt and sink into my thoughts in search of some way to relax. I think about women. I insert myself in a fantasy that I often indulge in where I'm the warden of an enormous women's prison that contains all the females I've most desired in my life. There's my geography teacher from junior high school years, and the delicious Monica, with the bell-shaped cheeks of her butt and her long, hairless legs, whom I treated so badly in the privacy of the bathroom. Also the television announcer, favorite heroine of my moist nights; the famous singer, the clerk in the office across the street. All isolated in tidy white rooms where the walls are decorated with Tolkienesque dragons (the presence of innocent sensuality), fields of bulblike flowers, and surrealistic curves dotted with penises that look like asteroids. Someday they'll find me naked among them. I'll say that someone threw me in there with them, and I'll put their lubricious appetite to the test, flooding their days with provocation until they concede me the glory of enjoying them at dusk and dawn, satisfying a hunger for bodies—their bodies— aged in my memory like the best of old port wines. On another floor of my prison I keep the flirts who have the souls of whores and the conduct of nuns, those prickteasers who save themselves for VIPs. Them I beat, and burn with wax—and burn myself too. I make them copulate with hounds and calves in the private rooms of young ladies with and without experience who consider themselves people of good taste. Sometimes I kill them. Just like that, when my depraved side can no longer accept seeing them reduced to beasts. Then I throw them in a dung heap of misfits, where they rot like the whores of hell. And all the while that I imagine all this, I'm restless and fidgety with the impossibility of doing it. I wouldn't do it even if it were real. It's a lecherous fit exacerbated by thirst, hunger, nausea, and my marvelous imagination. Could I be some hardly-ever-studied category of degenerate? I'm an emotional pervert, a temporary sadist who confronts the degeneracy of his libido in the midst of the debacle of his body. But desire itself can't be dirty, desire is never dirty, you just have to know how to socialize it...If I had to decide on the ideal woman, I'd be incapable of making the choice. For the girls who chase after tourists, I just have pity; they're good in bed, but they spoil the passion with their traumatic postcoital revelations. They end up mixing their lack of orgasms with politics. Communism is the cause of their frigidity. They're capable of spending a whole night expounding on who ends up with the surplus value they produce, as if the ideological question raised them above the rank of hooker. The rockers, on the other hand, are a bunch of cry-babies lamenting generational misunderstanding. They can't live with the model of a happy, hard-working, patriotic, love-song family that was promulgated in the seventies. In bed they tend to look for an escape from parental proscriptions, especially if they fornicate to the rock sounds of Testament or Creator. The bohemians and snobs care most about finding the metaphor of my sperm and then converting it into songs about the solitude of two within the collective. All that's left are the ones who have been integrated in the Revolution, the slogan girls, but now that I think of it, I realize I've never been with one of them.

MILE 64

It seems that the sea creatures have taken advantage of my lethargy to show themselves on the surface. Before it was the shark—which luckily has not returned—and now I awake to the splashing of a dolphin which passed right under the raft, performing a concert of squeals and squeaks in which I recognize the Flipper of my childhood. Maybe it will bring us a happy ending. Or maybe I'm just affected by its stereotypical image of kindness. I dreamed so many times of dolphins that saved me from killer whales and enormous and ferocious sharks. They were almost the only maritime attraction among my fantasies, because the sea never fascinated me at all. I was seldom happy at the beach, not even in adolescence when we used to go often. Those Sundays catching rays and downing soft drinks on the rough coral shore; savoring the cold sodas, the orange drink in quart bottles, the ice water from a thermos quenching the thirst born of puff pastries, bread with paté, greasy fried-dough delicacies soaked in syrup. After two dips in the water I tired of the food, the blazing sun, the salt that stuck to my skin. My body hurt and my clothes got rough like sandpaper, as if between flesh and cloth there were a thin film of sand, which in fact was nothing but tiny grains of salt...It's past twelve and the Commodore still hasn't woken up. His colossal form lies curled in a fetal position trying to keep the sun from reaching any spot left bare by the sheet which covers even his head. In any case he'll burn the same as me if the light really applies itself and cooks his hide so it's agonizing and incapable of resistance, stained with red blotches and dead layers...I look toward the horizon and can make out a strip which unnerves me, as the sky unnerves me with its unvarying litany. These have been days of sinister beauty, calm, there hasn't been a single cloud nor a wave to put us in danger. Everything keeps happening in complete environmental perfection. A stunning irony which hurts me when I remember how much I longed for a time like this: pure Parnassian harmony. And here it is, extinguishing us with mortal doses of blue sun. This isn't a mirage, it's an oppressive presence which will not go away and will persist in wounding me. But I don't want that, I'm just a painter, I don't deserve so much cruelty as this.

MILE 65

Worn out by torments that I won't repeat, I want to think about Cynthia, my sister, in fear that later on my physical decay will deny me the right to choose my reflections. Cynthia is a great girl, and she dealt with ten years of my causing trouble without anyone at home finding out. I paint because of her. She swore I'd be a talent, and this was enough for me to put up with six years between the still-lifes of the elementary and the abstractionist fever of San Alejandro. From there I would come to rest with a soliloquy expressing the vanity of the adolescent artist who wants to conquer the world. One day, in the house of a colleague, all of us infatuated with pyschodelia listening to "Dazed and Confused," someone pulled out a bundle wrapped in paper, and I learned to smoke marijuana. While I swallowed the smoke I remembered Cynthia who said I would be a great painter. From then on I would aspire to free up the myths rusted into the spiral of progress—to do battle with difficult subjects, believing myself the paladin of an art of essences. Until my sister cut off this path of quixotic poses, warning me that anyone who marginalizes himself by proclaiming himself anti-official is taking pride in a trickster's mask and an ephemeral idealism, because you can't have one revolution inside another. He who doesn't join up and criticize within the intimate ranks of its defenders becomes an opponent within the band of aged conspirators. Ambiguity—she added—is the heritage of opportunists who destroy History, whose commandments don't save them from becoming graveyards for lost souls; pure melancholia. I wanted to learn from her, the one who slept with whomever she liked, lived out her impulses, and the next morning got up, bestowed kisses on all the family, and graduated summa cum laude from the university. The day everyone least expected she filled her suitcase with clothes and books, carefully put away her bear Popote (bought nineteen years before as a level-three toy in the days of rationed Christmas presents) and bid us good-bye in the airport. She was one of the select few chosen to study for a master's in architecture in an American university. She promised her talented brother that she'd intercede on his behalf "so you can learn more about the other universe than you get from Saturday-night movies." She would do this with neither elation nor sensationalism, carefully feeling out what a land of immigrants would offer me. "If you're going to blow it in public, better you should stay here," she warned me with her serious expression. "I don't want to see you break your back for forty years and then try to convince me you succeeded because you've got a house with a yard, which might be something important to the majority of your acquaintances, but not to you. If you start thinking that way, even for a moment, then don't do it." The honest truth is that I was already thinking that way. The fucking house took the place of my creative longings and artist's dreams. As if each day I trusted less in my talent, as if I feared that over there things were too serious to play at being a painter, and the absence of Marxist edicts would rob all meaning from the sharp questioning in my work, which grew from my own universe of anarchy and ideological license; the remains of an arrogant adolescence spent in a country of placards. But before I could run to the cavern where St. Ignatius of Loyola fasted in expectation of a divine blessing, my sister woke everybody up with an early morning phone call that had us running in circles, "Daughter how are you? Speak up because we can't hear you this way!" That call of good omen converted the Commodore and myself into figures of the future; me with a scholarship at Stanford, and my brother-in-law as the "admiral" of a club in Rhode Island with a middle-class salary and a millionaire's tips. Right away dawns a day of joyful kisses and confused, impossible plans made on the spot; the house looks more beautiful and worrying becomes the weakness of a hypochondriac. My incurable reserve barred me from these excesses; I just smiled, eager to taste the forbidden capitalist fruit. And in the middle of that uproar, nobody remembered the visas which were as hard to acquire as an airplane trip itself—it was a moment when we said to hell with the whole situation of waiting lists and lines, television cut back to a half-day schedule, red beans and nothing else. But there was even more for me, when a week later I got the letter explaining everything, telling me about a sudden interest on the part of the imperial galleries in art by "Cubans from Cuba." To dispel any doubts, Cynthia enclosed an issue of *Newsweek* that reported on this unique new current, not yet even named, born of our creole paintbrushes and comparable only to the post-World War II avant-garde— with citations of very respected experts, for example, the critics of the *New York Times*. That was the apotheosis. Glittering parade of galas and receptions. Myself as the emperor of "know-how." The ease of enjoying a glory greater than that of the omnipotent president of "These United States." This time I couldn't contain my joy and so I resumed painting and believing in my sister's assumptions. The Commodore, for his part, seeing himself in the prologue to a comfortable and jubilant future, grew strident in his anticommunism, denouncing more than anyone a system of "contraptions and lunatics," as he liked to put it. He, who had been satisfied for so many years with the Saturday domino game, the bottle of ordinary rum (before the crisis of '89 with the supply of Yucayo), and Sundays at Guanabo beach, now puffed himself up to proclaim the redemption of his desires. Now he sees himself commanding twenty-meter yachts and wearing polo shirts as white as siren's breath. A rightwinger of a few months' standing, who doesn't know anything about ideology and never imagined himself a reformer nor smoked marijuana. A paradigm of official doctrine as long as it brought him a good life with New Year's at Varadero. A man who has made himself an unconscious victim of temporalities he doesn't understand. In Rome he would have been the stud-slave of dissolute princesses; in the Middle Ages, a good knight's squire; and here, in the last gasp of the millennium, he's an immigrant in search of an abundant country in which to found a race of hard-working men, bakers perhaps, who will protect themselves with the sign of the cross every time they hear the word *change*. In his place I don't know what I would have done if my companion on the voyage were to stupidly toss a knapsack full of canteens into the sea. I would take it as an act of genocide against my descendants, against a lineage which would take charge of spreading this axiom about the left throughout the world: that the left isn't just some notion of sex without marriage, no, that this notion of building an earthly utopia means a thousand pains and a thousand headaches, and really, it would be better to just leave things in their usual state. Therefore, on seeing all this placed at risk— if I were the Commodore—I'd come to the conclusion that in throwing the canteens into the sea my companion (me) committed an act of revolutionary vindication, assassinating an entire generation of potential anticommunists, and this would render twice as agonizing the suffering of these two final days. In thirst, dementia, hunger, and pain, I would see the nails which, with the passage of hours, were crucifying me upon this boat as a symbol of mistaken man.

MILE 66

When I moisten my lips with the tip of my tongue, I can feel how cracked they are. My throat burns from trying to swallow, it burns so much...

MILE 67

If I can't think of anything soon, I'll get delirious, I see it coming now...I'll recite poems, they say that Tomás Borge kept from going crazy in prison by reciting Rubén Darío from memory. I know it's not true because I read his book and they didn't beat him up that much. He even confessed to two or three things to avoid electrodes in his testicles and God knows what other evil antisubversive devices. He was brave enough to admit this, I don't blame him. But the method isn't a bad one, in any case. Repeating verses or songs or whatever, I can fight off derangement, although I don't know which to choose...I want something pleasant, not very complicated. Let's see...let's see...I don't remember any Vallejo or Neruda, Martí is who shows up first...I've loved Martí since I was a boy, and at home they had me memorize "The Little Pink Shoes" to recite to visitors. Now I've almost forgotten it, just a few stanzas come back to me:

> Bright sun and waves of froth—
> On the beach is young Pilar.
> Everyone knows she's come to show off
> Her new feathered hat from afar.
> Last night she dreamed of heaven,
> Was called by a song so grand,
> That I was so frightened and shaken,
> I brought her to sleep on the sand.
> Look, there's Alberto the soldier
> In his hat with corners three.
> On parade he looked so much older
> Now he launches a boat in the sea...

"The Two Princes" was always my favorite, it made me cry...I remember, I cried for the pain of both families, I recited it by heart:

> Among the forest poplars
> Lies the shepherd's home
> The shepherd's wife is asking
> "How can the sun still shine?"
> Heads down, the sheep are crowding
> All around the door
> They see the shepherd building
> A box so deep and long!
> In tears the shepherd picks up...

No, I think that doesn't come yet...

> A sad dog slips in and out,
> A voice sings in the house:
> "Oh birdie, I feel so crazy
> Take me where he flew!"
> In tears the shepherd picks up
> His shovel and his hoe
> In the ground a grave he opens
> And throws a flower within
> ...within...a flower...within
> No more son has the shepherd,
> The shepherd's son has died![14]

...think of another poem. Okay? Go on, think of another poem or a song, even if it's in English; even if it's the national anthem: *To com-bat run men of Ba-yaaamo so the nation can view you with priiiide don't fear the glory that will come if you've diiied to die for your country is to live to live in chains is to live under insults ground down hark to the bugle's sound to aaarms you brave ones run...I wanna give you my love I wanna give*

---

[14] These are fragments of "Los zapaticos de rosa" and "Los dos principes," the two most famous poems from Cuban poet José Martí's magazine for children, *La edad de oro*.

you my love whole lotta love whole lotta love...Very late very late the good things come first because the sun and then the water and meanwhile the owners and later the owners will put your dreams to death. And who said this? Who the hell said it?

MILE 68

Hold on, hold on, hold on, hold on...I don't stop telling myself, I chase after this phrase in my head; it hides behind a thousand mustard-yellow cups and indefinable sounds that begin to inundate me. The hallucinations—because that's what they are—barricade themselves behind my discomfort and they embody it too, they give life to the absurdity of my ills; desire to vomit is a boulder lodged in my belly, where it takes the place of my viscera and produces a heavy, glutted, stuffed need to get out. Nausea is a merry-go-round of which I'm the axle, it goes and goes revolving around my eyes full of red-painted children who yell at the top of their lungs, chanting unintelligible obscenities, screaming stupid songs that blend with my own memories. The little faces stick their tongues out at me and speak in tongues while they dance, they keep on dancing at the speed of a phonograph until their bodies are one body that simultaneously asks questions, talks, and yells from inside a mesh of purple streaks...Hold on, hold on. Just a day, a few hours, and everything will be over. Can't you even make a shitty little effort?...Hold on, damn it. Take another nitrazepam, pop five pills, sleep twenty hours and escape...escape...hold on and later you'll laugh till you burst remembering what you lived through on your voyage. Maybe in Hollywood they'll ask me to write a screenplay, they love these stories, I'll just have to change a few details. For instance, the Commodore would be a deserter from Cuban State Security, who is fleeing to the United States with a top-secret report which reveals that the Cubans, in revenge for the embargo, are planning a series of terrorist acts on cities in the U.S. All in cahoots with Palestinian intelligence, with Khadafy,

Saddam Hussein, and Chinese gangs in New York. I'd
be a double agent from Cuban counterintelligence,
charged with preventing the arrival of the document. Of
course, I fall in love with Sharon Stone and go over to
James Bond's side. The movie ends with the bad guys
committing suicide when they see their plans revealed,
and a presidential reception for the Commodore, Sharon,
and me. Just like in *Star Wars*, in an auditorium full of
senators, cabinet members, Arab princes and magnates
from Japan. It would be a box-office smash, and if it
doesn't happen, I'll move into comic books, I'm not a
painter for nothing...I just have to hold on. Holding on
is—here—not thinking about dying. Even if shivers are
shaking my bones, and cramps from dehydration bring
spasms, loss of judgment, whiplashes from a billion
nerves working for the continuation of pain. Every minute
that goes by, the worms are gaining ground. There are
cells that surrender to them without offering any resistance, and my body is a battlefield where I'm on the
weaker side. Necrosis advances, numbing my defenses,
surrounding my tissues with hunger and thirst. As a kid
I used to imagine this battle of the flesh when I got sick;
the antibiotics were the decisive reinforcements which
tipped the scales in my favor, they were my marshals
who arrived at the opportune moment, not like that Mar-
shal Grouchy who forgot his emperor at Waterloo. Now
I don't have any forces to throw into the battle, and more
than a confrontation of equals, it's a resistance struggle
in which my body desperately fights against its extinction, against domination by the worms who want to throw
a banquet on my carcass to glorify their latest kill. And
so, they're advancing along my arteries, galloping on
the toxins in my blood, infecting the reaches of my ten-
dons and larynx, the vessels that lead to my aorta and
later to the spinal cord and the skull where my last hopes
are hiding out. I don't know how long this might take,
but I'm well on the way to total defeat, and the only

thing that could prevent it would be the arrival of the People. Where are the People? What People, how many miles-hours-minutes are they away from me, or are there no People anywhere around me to help?...I have an external enemy: the sun and the sea...I have an internal enemy: the accursed worms, the organs that have already given up...One hope: the boat of the People..., four desperate variants: shoot myself, jump into the sea, drink the salt water, or cut open my veins...One fear: not to be able to go on.

MILE 69

The ghosts have arrived, and they're getting worse. They're bastards, because they didn't give any warning to the small scrap of reason I have left. Suddenly they're inside me, breaking down some door and leaving it open for the ones that want to finish driving me nuts. Millions and millions of noises...entertainment for the dying...the images come divided down the middle by a fine mist...my father converses with me, saying, "The nails in your window are broken, can you put in new ones, or does it have to wait until you're famous?" The universe is full of rocks...gray, cold rocks covered with green slime. A long passage opens, almost completely dark, with a muddy, sloping floor. On both sides are little passageways that lead to an icy lake populated by blind fish. But I don't want to think of water...I'm fleeing, running to the end of the labyrinth where I come to rest in front of an intense light that makes me cover my eyes. After an instant I glimpse a huge green meadow that's been mowed as neatly as a soccer field. There are no trees or houses or people, only the green grass and blue sky...I take one step forward and the carpet sinks under my weight, plunging me into a foam as white as milk...I'm immersed in a silver ocean among reflections of the clouds of my earliest days. I drink it and find it delicious, and I'll keep drinking while I swim through its liquid prairies...Here there's no sun, the light is mild-mannered in spite of its strength, and it fades with the passage of time. Then come the shadows, the white ocean ceases to exist and I'm overtaken by an aggressive sea that claws out my insides as my body shakes with death-rattle spasms...Shouts echo inside me, proclaiming to the worms that the end of the Supreme Vertebrate is near...Faces on all sides, the bustle of the streets, the train that used to go by...mommy, do beaches sleep?...*She is buying a stairway to heaven...Heaven, I'm in heaven*... And Gagarin said that the moon was a lovely blue ball, and Neil Armstrong never went to the moon...two thousand, one hundred and ninety Cubans dead in Africa, Uncle Julian told me this morning when he came back from the cemetery...Europe is sinking, Asia is exploding with technology, and America is the great whore upon the beast described by the apostle John...The news of the most recent weeks is arriving as well as that of ten and twelve years ago. A red ribbon announces that Tamayo[15] arrived in outer space with a bottle full of sand from Playa Giron.[16] Mama cries for the six Cubans sacrificed alongside the single-starred banner during the invasion of Grenada. Then it turns out to be a lie...I see my father dressed in a suit for my sister's sweet fifteen, but she doesn't want a party, nor any photos taken of her next to a pot of gladiolas, or of her emerging from the bathtub in a bathing suit, or admiring herself in the mirror, or stretched out in a double bed disguised as Gilberta Swann. She'd prefer to go with me and drink Carta Blanca on the roof of a very tall building, very tall...my grandparents in Batabanó have taken me to see a two-headed pig. It's a horror. How terrible to be born with two heads, to be required to look constantly at what surrounds you; it's overpowering reality, hyperrealism, anti-escape...Nobody needs to be born that way, it's better to close your eyes and give yourself over to the colored circles of the deepest dark...I cover my face but the silhouettes of air and smoke are still there, the spirits shout at me...Cynthia offers a toast to my health and says smiling: "May you go far, Tiziano." I need a break. This is another move made by my bad

---

[15] Tamayo: a Cuban cosmonaut, the first Latin American in space.
[16] Playa Giron: the beach where the Bay of Pigs invaders landed and were defeated.

side. Do they think they can fool me? Here there are no
faces or voices or any fucking thing; they're ideas, pure
ideas, they're not voices, they're ideas
                voices
        ideas
                        ideas
                        ideas
                                voices
                                ideas
hand me the canteen
                                        voices
                                        the service sucks
voices
        voices
voicesideasvoicesvoicesvoicesvoicesvoicesvoicesvoices
ideas
            idea
shut up
please
ideas
 ideas
                                        voices
                                        what happened is that I
put my foot in it
                                        up to my balls
no more than two days
                                        ideas
                                                voices
the beautiful house with a garden

sixty-foot yachts
            Cuba would be the South Korea of the Americas

    there's something up there
a system of contraptions and lunatics
                                            it has to do
with hope

voices

    voices

        voices

            voices

                voices

I wanna give you my love I wanna give you my love whole lotta love whole lotta love ta'tatatata' tatata' tatata' ta'tatatata' tatata' tatata' *whole lotta love whole lotta love* uuuuuuuhhhhhh!...music...the marvel of music, coming to me the way I deserve...The true pleasures of the mirage—the melodies in crescendo sounding at your request. Here are the ballads for virgins and the heavy metal of "fuck off" and "motherfucker"...Come on, come on epic sounds, the bang-bang-bang music criticized by my mother...Come on Pink Floyd, let me hear you and remember that "comfortably numb," yes I hear the bombs as they fall, and I know about walls, and lambs and candles hidden for bad times...Come on, a thousand nights of opera and the *presto* of a Vivaldian summer. Do you see? My wires are crossed, this much madness frightens me...Four horsemen come galloping toward me, and behind them a fifth, whose gait disturbs me...Guitars, guitars, guitars, we're going "trashing"...Shit. Don't they understand there's someone dying here? Don't they have an ounce of respect? Get rid of them, with all their bullshit! I want to be alone...! Leave me in peace...Ozzy, *please*, teach me, go on, teach me to close my eyes forever...

MILE 70

I just drank my own urine. The warm, bit-
ter liquid came back to me to fool the silly cells that are
out on strike, and I can feel some slight improvement so
they must have swallowed it. What is this called...a coun-
teroffensive? The repugnant taste of urine is doubly dis-
gusting when it comes from a body which is rotting
alive...Three tablets of nitrazepam went along with it.
The sleeping pills will go on distancing the defeat of my
flesh...The Commodore is talking. First word since yesterday and it's to tell me that if nothing shows up tomorrow he's going to shoot himself with one of the bullets
left from his sea gull "hunt." His voice was sluggish but
convincing...I was surprised at the fear I felt when I lis-
tened, when it's supposed that death is imminent, there's
no reason to react that way to a logical solution, which
demonstrates that I'm still not giving up. I'm committed
to going all the way, I can't shoot myself...even if my
desperation grows a thousand times worse than all the
desperations I'm living through now.

SEVENTH DAY
2:13 AM

MILE 75

At times, only at times, I recover my wits through my nose—the smell of the sea, the smell of deepest night...Where could we be? Far, the Commodore said one night...Night isn't over. I can feel the sea rising; the rolling is stronger, and after every three or four little waves comes a huge one that completely drenches us in heavy, cold water. Maybe there's a storm approaching, and I don't care...it's all the same to me, a hurricane or a dead calm, because both of them kill without consideration of who might be adrift...And I used to think I'd die in a hospital, old and surrounded by a hypocritical family waiting for my final sigh...I'll be an anonymous corpse, a plaything of politicians, maybe a martyr...The tomb of the unknown rafter...Didn't the Commodore say something about a storm? The ocean is getting worse...The woman who would have been my wife won't ever know I existed. She'll be somebody else's wife, married to some usurper living in my place without even knowing that he's supplanted me, that his children should have been mine...At least I lived, being born is a stroke of luck, being chosen, me...Another wave, shit! Foam, cold, and the wind is whipping now, rising along with the sound of the white-capped sea...I enjoyed good women and forbidden pleasures...Within the span of twenty years, the work I am leaving behind will transform me into the necessary Christ of the maladjusted....We're sliding over the waves, down the slopes that separate the peaks...The howling gets louder, and as we crash against these dark bodies we're losing ourselves in the salt sea...I clutch desperately onto the hand-hold of the raft and yell for the Commodore to do the same although I don't know whether he hears me...His body is a lifeless mass that at any minute will be taken by the waves...My only consolation is that sooner or later those who are alive today will be joining me, I'd only be losing sixty or so years of mortality, that's all...Why am I spouting all this idiocy?...This isn't happening to me...I don't want to surrender my body to the worms...I don't want to, and I'll curse my country and I'll curse the Americans...the world ought to blow up like this: BLAM! so that everything's done with. My god, how much I want to cry!

MILE 76

I don't know what time it is, but dawn must have come by now. There's no sun...my eyes can't make out anything but broad colors, and the color of the sky moving overhead is dark. It's the dim color of the great clouds that have arrived to finish us off...The wind wails unbearably...*The Social Contract* continues to fight off the sea, her stern confronts mountains of water, she rises on the crest and falls immediately into the abyss between liquid walls but she doesn't let herself get trapped. Through the salty deluge, her prow and I both rear up and then slip down...The Commodore seems dumb-struck, I've got my feet braced against his shoulders and I can't feel any reaction on his part, as if he doesn't care about getting through this...I can't be so docile, they're going to have to tear me from the raft...up...up we go, one two three...Doooown! Blows, pushes, shoves, turns and more turns...It's raining...a tremendous downpour is falling on us...This has got to be the center of the storm...The waves feel weaker...two go by, four, five, six; the raft starts to drop, I hear a roar...I feel it closing in, the crest curling and breaking, the one that's looking for us...in mid-air...Tons of water explode over me...I'm swallowing seawater through my mouth, my ears, my eyes, my pores...I'm drowning...we're sinking...another instant and on the surface again...it's incredible they don't smash us...shadows, moving shadows...Salt gushes out of me, I'm fainting...Don't let go, don't! Hold on...Someone's screaming, he says it's all over. My screams are mixed with the Commodore's—nobody else is proclaiming the right to euthanasia, if that's what you can call death by seven days of agony, a death that doesn't offer a painless way of perishing, but instead forces the life cycle of a debilitated soul to end. And he, suddenly awake, pleads that we should let go. I insist on holding on...here comes the next big wave, and little by little the Colossus gets up from the floor of the raft...I don't ask him to steady himself, he's made his decision now...We start the descent...I can see the solid wall of ocean that we're going to smash up against...I hear it whistle in a crescendo...The white whirlpool hurls itself in search of *The Social Contract*...I tighten my fists around the handhold, hold my breath, and take a final look at my fellow traveler on this voyage. He swears something that gets lost in the terrible impact...Water, water, water, water, and more water falling over me...Is this the end? Water, water...I can't stand another second without air...I don't feel my body...water...pushes, shoves, and... Upward!...air, air, I'm afloat, spinning, the raft rears up and frees itself of all the accumulated water, it's light and floating all over again...The Commodore is no longer on board, the Gulf took him...He's dead...Cynthia from now on you're a widow, at twenty-nine you lost your man in an unknown little corner of the world...I swear to you, I'll keep going, I'm not surrendering to a yellow cup or a scrambled sea. Your brother is standing up to the worst, and if after so much effort I don't succeed, I can at least enjoy the thought that I didn't save those shitty worms a single day of work...Cynthia, is it true I would have been a good painter? The Commodore ran out of ideas, he was heading for a rendezvous with white yachts, but none appeared at the necessary hour...The white yachts did not appear...I was left alone, all alone...it's raining...don't stop letting your sweet water fall...the waves...the wind...spinning, spinning...up...silence...and doooown...uuuuup...air, air...waves, rain, spin, spin, my hands hurt...only a little more...don't let go...everything's spinning around me, I think I'm going to black out...my hands...no...no I can't hear...I'm gone...I'm gone...Cynthia, I'm suffering things you can't imagine, one day I'll tell you about them.

MILE 85

I'm not dead yet. The sun is shining full on my face, and that's the only sensation I have that allows me to infer the presence of light. There are no external sounds; aren't the million festive drumrolls and amorphous voices lodged in my brain enough? My brain matter, on which my worms—finally—have begun to feed. They're eating my nightmares, soon they'll drink from the yellow cup, and then, to my relief, I'll cease to exist for good.

MILE 86

I'm going to drink the sea...

MILE 87

I'm going to drink the sea...

MILE 88

I'm vomiting up all my organs, out comes bloody frothy stuff mixed with the last of my yellow waste matter. Millions of worms are escaping through what my throat is giving back...I hear it fall on the now-peaceful surface of the water...I'm vomiting again...I've got the shakes all over and I spit blood, my eyes don't see but I recognize the taste of this refuse on my tongue. It's getting cold, and at the same time I'm getting free of the pain...No more thirst, no more hunger...Is there anything left inside me?...I'm blacking out...Here comes the labyrinth of mossy rocks, back again; the place is dark and icy cold. I proceed as if I were levitating, somewhere far ahead there must be a way out, a lighted opening that I saw before, that's where the silvery ocean is...I have to get there...not much further...No, suddenly I don't want to go ahead...I don't want to die...it's at the end of the tunnel...help me stop...I have to go back...help me, damn it...don't leave me...come here, come close to me, don't leave me alone because I think I'm dying...do something...hold me by the arms and push me outside...I want a hand, I want to feel something warm and alive against my flesh...whatever ...anything warm I can hold onto...hurry up, damn it, I'm running out of time...don't leave me alone...no...no, this light is a trick...and it's coming so close...a hand...Isn't there one lousy hand able to get me out of here? They're pulling me toward the light...stop...oh, damn, please stop...Why don't you let me go back where I belong?...even for a minute...don't leave me...the corridor is running out...there's no more time...My god, there's no more time...it's ending...it's ending...I'm descending...I'm descending...

MILE 89

Is there anybody here? It seems this is the end of the voyage. Now I can speak about myself. I suppose I'm a corpse....It's no worse than I thought, it's possible to endure defeat. My fate is to go on travelling who knows how much longer through the sea, later they'll have to put me right into a plastic bag, and from there to a hole in foreign ground. Death doesn't end everything, it's a healthy and perennial peace in which I could very patiently await the arrival of my saviors. Now there's no need for you to hurry, I can wait for you another week, or a few years, even a century. Perhaps when I wake up I'll discover that the world has been fixed, that the Tower of Babel has reached heaven at last. No, no such dreams. Better that they never find me, or at least not in the next few millennia. I belong to the sea.

MILE 90

DATE DUE

#45220 Highsmith Inc. 1-800-558-2110